I0821883

U-420

U-420

ISBN: 979-8-9907254-5-4 (hardback)
979-8-9907254-4-7 (paperback)

Printed in the United States of America

U-420

GARY J. ROSE

DEDICATION

First and foremost, I thank God for blessing me with the gift of imagination and the ability to craft a thrilling story to entertain readers.

To my sister, Debbie Miller, for her unwavering support and meticulous first review of the manuscript, catching my errors and helping to bring this novel to life.

To my loyal Jeannie Loomis fans, thank you for your enthusiasm and support in following her adventures.

And to my horror novel fans, I appreciate your love for the spine-chilling tales and your continued encouragement.

History is hardly littered with
good examples of destruction leading
smoothly to regeneration.

The Guardian (2016)

PROLOGUE

By late 1944 and early 1945, the Nazi military force was collapsing, and Nazi troops were forced to retreat on all fronts. Despite the clear impending defeat of Nazi Germany, thousands of concentration camp prisoners continued to perish. The monstrous machinery of the "final solution" kept operating until the very last moment, even as the extensive empire of Nazi concentration camps had already collapsed.

The Nazis were desperately trying to cover up their crimes. In 1943, they liquidated evidence of mass murder during Operation Reinhard in Treblinka, Sobibor, Belzec, and Majdanek. In October 1944, on Himmler's orders, traces of the murders at Auschwitz were destroyed, and the gas chambers were blown up. Auschwitz was liberated by the Red Army on January 27, 1945.

Hitler was obsessed with a "bigger is better" mentality, often wasting resources Germany could scarcely afford. The devastating use of the V1 and V2 rockets and the cutting-edge use of jet engines on planes are two examples. However, the V2s lacked pinpoint accuracy or giant warheads, making them less of a critical threat. The jet planes faced issues with insufficient fuel and trained pilots to effectively deploy the fighters they had.

Hitler also focused on bigger and better tanks. Although superior to both American and Russian tanks, the diverse range of German tanks caused logistical problems in the field. When one broke down, scavenging parts from another damaged unit was extremely difficult. Hitler ignored concerns about production costs, manpower usage, and the practicality of the equipment in battle.

As more was learned about German preparations and progress with new weapons, it became clear that the Allies had ended the war with Germany just in time. The dangers faced, especially by Britain, were numerous and severe.

German innovations included radio and optical equipment, such as infra-red searchlights used in conjunction with the 88mm gun to blind and destroy tanks moving at night. There were rocket-assisted shells where rockets provided further propulsion after the shell was launched, and there were plans to equip V2 rockets with wings for greater effectiveness.

In chemical warfare, the Germans had developed a new, highly lethal gas in large quantities. While it could have been countered, it would have caused significant trouble and loss due to lax anti-gas discipline in England. Hitler personally prevented its use, not out of altruism, but because he doubted its efficacy.

The Germans experimented with a piloted VI flying bomb for greater accuracy and made progress with controlled projectiles for targeting ground targets or aircraft. Hitler also shifted his focus to naval construction when he realized the war was lost. Innovations included an 80-mile range torpedo with an acoustic head and controlled torpedoes with deadly potential. They also developed a jet-propelled submarine capable of 25 knots underwater, made possible by new fuel.

These inventions were in various stages of development, from pre-development to full production. The Germans prepared to carry out all essential production in underground factories impervious to bombing, illustrating the full extent of the peril.

The Germans, however, were transitioning to a different kind of warfare, and many of their new developments could have been as deadly as those already known, like the VI and V2 rockets. While Allied bombing delayed this transition and hampered development, especially through attacks on communications, it could not stop it entirely.

Alongside his scorched earth policy, initially entrusted to Albert Speer, Hitler had a particularly sinister revenge weapon in mind—one that would further his desire for the Third Reich to endure even after his death.

This weapon, code-named "Erneuerung" (a German word for "renewal"), was authorized by Hitler himself. He envisioned a modern nuclear submarine, unparalleled in its capabilities, surpassing any submarine of any nation, even by today's standards.

But Hitler's vision went beyond mere technological superiority. Leveraging Nazi advancements in cryonics, German scientists perfected the ability to place submariners in suspended animation.

This groundbreaking technology meant that the crew and the futuristic U-boat could lie dormant for an extended period, only to re-emerge when the time was right to wreak havoc on the nations that had destroyed the Third Reich.

Hitler's plan was as ambitious as it was terrifying. The Erneuerung submarine, equipped with state-of-the-art weaponry and manned by a crew preserved through cryonic suspension, was intended to be a hidden threat lying in wait beneath the ocean's surface.

Decades or even centuries after the fall of Nazi Germany, this vessel would resurface, unleashing a devastating surprise attack on an unsuspecting world. This notion of a vengeful resurgence from the depths added a chilling new dimension to the already horrifying legacy of the Third Reich, embodying Hitler's relentless pursuit of power and domination, even from beyond the grave.

U-Boat 420 Operation Erneuerung

CHAPTER 1

BERLIN, APRIL 1945

The once-grand city now lay in ruins, shrouded in smoke and littered with rubble. The sound of distant explosions and the constant rumble of artillery fire filled the air, a relentless reminder of the war's devastation. In the heart of this chaos lay the Führerbunker, a concrete fortress beneath the crumbling city.

Inside the Führerbunker, the atmosphere was tense and suffocating. Dimly lit corridors were filled with anxious officers and frantic aides, moving with a sense of urgency and desperation. Adolf Hitler paced back and forth in his private office, his face a mask of fury and despair. His hair was disheveled, and his eyes were wild with a mix of rage and fear. Before him stood Dr. Helmut Krieger, a man of cold intellect and steely resolve, clutching a dossier tightly.

"The war is lost, Krieger," Hitler's voice trembled with anger. "The Allies are at our doorstep, and our defenses are crumbling. We need a plan—something that can ensure the survival of the Reich, even if we fall."

Dr. Krieger nodded, his voice steady. "My Führer, we have been working on a solution. Our scientists have developed a cryonics chamber capable of preserving our finest soldiers in a state of suspended animation. We can place them in this state, inside the Erneuerung submarine in Bergen. Both the submarine and crew can lay dormant until sometime in the future. They can be awakened ready to continue our mission."

Hitler's eyes narrowed, a glimmer of hope appearing in his gaze. "How soon can this be implemented?"

"The submarine is prepared, and the chambers are ready. All we need is your order, and we can proceed immediately," Krieger replied with determination.

Hitler stopped pacing, staring intently at Krieger while holding his shaking arm. The room fell silent, the weight of the decision hanging heavily in the air. Finally, he nodded decisively. "Do it. Ensure that the Third Reich endures. The world will not forget us."

Dr. Krieger bowed slightly and exited the room, leaving Hitler to his thoughts. The sounds of war raged on outside as the scene faded to black.

BERGEN, NORWAY

The hidden submarine base, carved into the fjords, was a stark contrast to the chaos in Berlin. The facility was a hub of activity, with scientists and engineers working tirelessly to prepare the advanced U-boat for its mission. The sleek, dark hull of the submarine gleamed under the harsh lights of the cavernous tunnel. Admiral Karl Weiss stood on the deck, overseeing the final preparations with a stern expression.

Inside the submarine, the atmosphere was a mix of nervous anticipation and meticulous precision. Crew members, dressed in crisp uniforms, moved with purpose as they loaded supplies and equipment. The cryonics chambers, sleek and futuristic, were being installed and calibrated under the watchful eye of Dr. Krieger. Captain Hans Bauer stood nearby, his face etched with skepticism.

Admiral Weiss went below to the cryonics chambers and found Dr. Krieger and Captain Bauer in deep conversation. Overhearing what was said, the Admiral waited for the opportune time to interrupt the two.

Dr. Krieger looked intently at Hans, who was clearly struggling to grasp the concept. "Hans, imagine if you could simply sleep through the years, untouched by time, and wake up exactly the same as when you fell asleep. That is essentially what hypersleep, or cryonic suspension, aims to achieve."

Hans nodded slowly, his curiosity piqued.

"Hypersleep is a state where biological processes are slowed down to a near halt," Dr. Krieger continued. "By drastically lowering the body's temperature and carefully managing the body's functions, we can preserve individuals for extended periods without the typical wear and tear of aging. In this state, metabolism is reduced to a minimal level, almost like pressing a pause button on life itself."

"How is that possible, Dr. Krieger?" Hans asked, still trying to wrap his mind around the concept.

"It's all about controlling the environment," Dr. Krieger explained. "We use advanced cryogenic technology to create and maintain these conditions. Specially designed chambers ensure that the body is kept at an optimal temperature, and a precise mixture of chemicals prevents ice crystals from forming in the cells, which could cause damage. This state of suspended animation can be maintained for years, even decades."

Hans's eyes widened. "So, the crew will be frozen in time?"

"Not frozen in the traditional sense," Dr. Krieger corrected. "Think of it more as being placed in a deep, dreamless sleep. Their bodily functions are slowed to such an extent that aging is almost entirely halted. When the time comes, we can gradually reverse the process, warming them up and reactivating their metabolic functions. They would wake up feeling as though no time had passed at all."

Hans glanced at the futuristic U-boat, then back at Dr. Krieger. "And we'll be ready to continue the fight?"

Dr. Krieger nodded solemnly. "Exactly. When the right moment arrives, you'll awaken, fully rested and prepared to carry out their mission. It's Hitler's way of ensuring that the Third Reich has a future, even if it means waiting in the shadows for the right time to strike."

Hans shivered, not from the cold, but from the sheer audacity of the plan. The idea of soldiers lying dormant, waiting to unleash havoc upon the world, was both terrifying and awe-inspiring.

"I know you have doubts, Hans," Admiral Weiss said while also looking at Captain Bauer, his voice steady. "But this is our only hope. The Führer has entrusted us with the future of the Reich."

He will follow orders, Admiral," Captain Bauer interjected. "But I can't help but wonder if we're grasping at straws. This cryonics technology—it's untested, unproven. What if something goes wrong?"

"We must have faith in our scientists and in the Führer's vision. Our mission is of utmost importance. We cannot afford to fail," Weiss reassured him, clasping Bauer's shoulder.

Dr. Krieger smiled, his expression one of determination and pride. He inspected the cryonics chambers, ensuring that every detail was perfect. He turned to the assembled crew of U-Boat 717, his eyes gleaming with anticipation. "You are about to embark on a journey beyond imagination," he addressed them, his voice echoing in the cavernous space. "Remember, you carry the future of the Reich in your hands. You will awaken in a new world, a world where the ideals of the Reich can be reborn in a U-Boat the world has never seen."

Admiral Karl Weiss stepped forward, his presence commanding attention. "Indeed, this is no ordinary submarine," he began, his voice filled with pride as he looked about. "U-Boat 420, bearing the Fuhrer's birthday, is a marvel of engineering, far ahead of its time. It is equipped with an experimental nuclear reactor, providing it with unparalleled underwater endurance and speed. It has a stealth mechanism that makes it virtually impossible to hear or track. This advanced stealth technology will keep our enemies blind to our approach, and invisible to sonar detection."

He continued, his voice growing more animated. "The hull is reinforced with an alloy developed in our most secret laboratories, making it impervious to depth charges and torpedoes. We possess a cutting-edge navigation system that ensures precise control, even in the most treacherous waters. Our weaponry is unmatched, with torpedoes that can strike targets from distances previously thought impossible. This

U-Boat is the epitome of German innovation and ingenuity."

The crew members exchanged uneasy glances but nodded in agreement, their resolve hardening with each word. The magnitude of their mission began to sink in, and they stood taller, ready to face the future.

Admiral Weiss continued, his voice filled with anticipation. "We are going to take her out shortly and put her through various maneuvers—stretch her legs, so to speak. You might be wondering why this is necessary since you will soon join her in a frozen time capsule. This is true, but it is essential that you familiarize yourselves with every nuance of how she runs.

Your memories will retain the information about her capabilities and performance, ensuring that when you awaken, you will be fully prepared to navigate and utilize this advanced vessel to its fullest potential. This exercise is crucial for your acclimatization and for the success of our future mission. Heil Hitler!"

The crew snapped to attention and responded with "Heil Hitler" and gave the Nazi salute.

The submarine's engines roared to life, a deep, resonant hum that filled the tunnel. The vessel began to move slowly forward, its sleek form cutting through the water with ease. The mission, shrouded in secrecy and hope, was now underway. The submarine disappeared into the depths of the tunnel, the harsh lights fading as darkness enveloped the vessel.

The sounds of the base grew distant, replaced by the eerie silence of the underwater world, where U-Boat 420 would soon lie in wait, its crew preserved for a future yet to come. The war for them would not continue until 2024.

CHAPTER 2

After finishing her trial run, the atmosphere inside the submarine was tense and clinical. Crew members stood in a line, each waiting their turn for the cryonics procedure. Dr. Krieger and his team of scientists moved with practiced efficiency, checking monitors and adjusting settings on the cryonics chambers. The hum of machinery and the soft beeping of monitors filled the air.

Admiral Weiss stood watching the process take place. His expression stoic. Captain Bauer stepped into the first cryonics chamber, lying down on the sleek, padded surface. "Good luck Captain. Happy hunting," Admiral Weiss said, as Dr. Krieger adjusted the controls, and a hiss of cold vapor surrounded the Captain as the chamber sealed shut. His breath fogged the glass, and his eyes slowly closed as the cryonics process took effect. One by one, the crew members underwent the procedure.

Once the crew of U-boat 420 was in hyper-sleep, Admiral Weiss approached Dr. Krieger. "Herr Doctor, no one has asked you how, in the future, the crew will be awakened from their hypersleep," he said.

Dr. Krieger gave a slight nod, a knowing smile playing on his lips. "Admiral, the process is designed to be as seamless as possible. When the time is right, an automated system will initiate the reanimation sequence. The chambers are equipped with advanced sensors that monitor the crew's vital signs continuously. These sensors are programmed to detect specific environmental cues or pre-set time intervals."

He paused, making sure Weiss was following. "In the event of an emergency, a manual override can be activated remotely by our successors- those of the Reich who survive. The chambers will gradually increase the crew's body temperature and restart their metabolic processes. They will wake up feeling as though they had just taken a long, dreamless nap, ready to carry out their mission."

Weiss looked thoughtful, then nodded. "Thank you, Herr Doctor. Let's hope everything goes according to plan."

The scientists completed the final checks. The lights dimmed, and the chambers emitted a soft, eerie glow as the crew entered a state of suspended animation. The submarine's systems switched to low power mode, the hum of the engines fading into silence.

Remotely the submarine was submerged, nestled in the dark, cold waters outside one of the U-boat bunkers in the Bergen tunnel. The vessel lay in wait, hidden from the world, its crew preserved in a timeless sleep.

BERGEN, NORWAY, 2024

The modern research vessel, the Arctic Explorer, cut through the water near Bergen, Norway, its equipment bristling with advanced technology. It just passed the Nazi U-boat bunker known as 'Bruno' one of their crucial bases for operations in the North Atlantic.

In all, the Germans had five other major U-boat bunkers. In France, Saint-Nazaire was one of the largest U-boat bases on the Atlantic coast. The base had extensive facilities and was heavily fortified.

The second of three U-boat bases was in Lorient, France. It was equipped with large concrete pens to protect the submarines from aerial attacks.

The third base in France, was in Brest. It was a significant base with massive bunkers to shield U-boats from Allied bombing raids.

La Rochelle, France, had a fortified submarine base with substantial protective structures. It was similar in construction to the U-boat bunkers in Hamburg, Germany. But the Third Reich loved to utilize the massive U-boat bunker in Bergen, Norway. Code named Bruno, it was a crucial base for operations in the North Atlantic.

BERGEN, NORWAY. CODE NAME "BRUNO."

After the Arctic Explorer docked next to the former U-boat bunkers, Dr. Lena Lawrence collected her specimens and left the ship. She made her way to the small bedroom in the research center to change her clothes. At 5'8", the shapely blonde often drew attention, and today was no exception. Her presence turned heads as she entered the research building, her confident stride commanding the room's respect.

Her graduate assistant, Alina Cretu, an athletic Romanian tech wiz, greeted her warmly as soon as she stepped inside. Alina's dark hair was tied back in a practical ponytail, her eyes sparkling with enthusiasm.

"Find anything of interest?" Alina asked, her face lighting up with a huge smile.

Lena returned the smile, shaking her head slightly. "Nothing earth-shattering, but we won't know for sure until we put them under the microscope. The real work starts now."

Together, they moved toward the lab, their footsteps echoing in the spacious, high-tech facility. The anticipation of discovery hung in the air, fueling their determination and focus. The sterile environment of the lab, with its gleaming surfaces and sophisticated equipment, was a stark contrast to the rugged exterior of the research center.

As they reached the lab door, Lena turned to Alina with a grateful smile. "Why don't you go ahead and start cleaning up the specimens? I'm going to take a quick shower and change into some warm clothes. Plus, I am in desperate need of a hot cup of coffee."

Alina nodded, her eyes twinkling with understanding. "Of course, Lena. Take your time. I'll get everything prepped and ready for you."

Lena watched as Alina moved with practiced efficiency, setting up the equipment and laying out the specimens. With a final appreciative glance, Lena headed towards the showers, the promise of warmth and caffeine motivating her tired limbs.

"I thought I might find you here, Dr. Lena Lawrence, runner-up for the Nobel Prize in Marine Biology," a cheerful voice called out. Dr. Alex Sousa approached with a smile, holding a cup of coffee as he sat down beside her.

"Well, if it isn't Dr. Alex Sousa, our resident World War II historian," Lena replied teasingly. She took a sip of her coffee, the warmth of the cup contrasting with the cool sea breeze.

Alex settled down next to her, his eyes scanning the surroundings. "I just love it here in these bunkers," Lena continued. "I know the history behind them. I should feel shocked or disturbed, but I don't. There's something about the smell of the sea air, the cry of the gulls, and the echoes of the past. I can almost imagine the energy that must have once filled this place."

Alex nodded, appreciating her sentiment. "It's fascinating how history and nature intertwine here. These bunkers, once symbols of conflict, now stand as silent witnesses to the passage of time. They're part of the landscape, part of the story."

Lena looked at him, her eyes sparkling with enthusiasm. "Exactly. It's like these bunkers have absorbed the essence of everything that's happened here. The battles, the tension, the moments of peace. It's all woven into the fabric of this place."

Alex took a sip of his coffee, savoring the moment. "And now, they're a part of our story too. Two scientists, each with our own passions, finding common ground in the remnants of the past."

Lena smiled, feeling a sense of camaraderie. "It's funny how life brings people together in the most unexpected places. Who would have thought that a marine biologist and a World War II historian would find so much to talk about?"

Alex chuckled. "Well, history and biology aren't as different as they seem. Both are about understanding the world, uncovering the truth, and connecting the dots."

Lena nodded thoughtfully. "You're right. And maybe that's why I feel so connected to this place. It's like standing on the edge of history, looking out at the vast ocean of possibilities."

The two sat in comfortable silence for a moment, each lost in their own thoughts. The sea breeze rustled through the old bunkers, carrying with it the distant calls of seagulls and the rhythmic sound of waves crashing against the shore.

Alex broke the silence, his tone soft and reflective. "It's moments like these that remind me why I chose to study history. It's not just about the past; it's about understanding how the past shapes the present and the future."

Lena glanced at him, her expression serene. "And for me, it's about understanding the delicate balance of marine ecosystems, how every organism plays a role in the grand tapestry of life. We're both seekers of knowledge, in our own ways."

Alex smiled warmly. "Here's to the seekers, then. May our journeys be filled with discovery and wonder."

As they clinked their cups together, a sense of shared purpose and friendship settled between them. In the quiet solitude of the bunkers, surrounded by the whispers of history and the call of the sea, Dr. Lena Lawrence and Dr. Alex Sousa found a connection that would carry them through the challenges and adventures that lay ahead.

As Alina busied herself with the specimens, another researcher, Dr. Mark Thompson, entered the lab. He was a tall man in his early forties, with a neatly trimmed beard and an inquisitive look in his eyes. He glanced outside the window facing the U-boat bunkers and noticed a man sitting next to Dr. Lena.

"Hey Alina," Mark said, nodding towards the man. "Who's that sitting next to Dr. Lena?"

Alina looked up from her work and followed his gaze. She smiled when she saw who he was referring to. "Oh, that's Dr. Alex Sousa," she replied. "He's a World War II historian. He got in late last night."

Mark raised an eyebrow, intrigued. "World War II historian? What brings him here?"

Alina leaned against the lab counter, her expression brightening as she spoke about Alex. "Alex has been collaborating with us on this project. He's here to help us understand the historical significance of the

U-boat bunkers and any artifacts we might find. His knowledge is incredible. He's been studying these bunkers for years and knows every detail about their construction and use during the war."

Mark nodded, clearly impressed. "That's fascinating. I can see how his expertise would be invaluable, especially given the historical context of our research."

Alina continued, "Absolutely. He's also a great person to work with. Always willing to share his knowledge and provide insights that we might overlook. Dr. Lena really enjoys working with him, and I think they make a great team."

Mark glanced back at Alex, now deep in conversation with Lena. "I can see that. It must be interesting to have someone with such a different background contributing to our work."

"It is," Alina agreed, her eyes returning to her task. "It's a reminder that science and history are often more interconnected than we realize. And who knows what we might discover with his help."

"I don't know though. My gut tells me that there is a little spark between them," Mark said followed by a wink.

Alina got up and looked out the window. "You think?"

CHAPTER 3

Admiral Weiss stood at the edge of the deep pit inside the U-boat bunker, his stern gaze fixed on the activity below. Workers, thin and gaunt, moved methodically under the watchful eyes of armed guards. These Jewish concentration camp prisoners worked with a grim efficiency, aware that their lives depended on the speed and accuracy of their labor. Their efforts were monitored by heavily armed SS soldiers.

The sleek hull of U-boat 420 lay submerged in the pit, a silent sentinel waiting for its time to come. The cryonics chambers inside held their precious cargo in suspended animation, the crew oblivious to the world outside. Weiss's heart was heavy with the weight of his responsibility; ensuring that the submarine remained hidden until the designated time was crucial to their mission.

He turned to the foreman, a burly man with a serious expression. "Make sure the cement is poured evenly and thoroughly. There can be no mistakes,"

Weiss commanded, his voice carrying the authority of his rank.

"Yes, Admiral," the foreman replied, nodding firmly. He signaled to the workers, and they began the process, the thick, gray mixture flowing steadily from the hoses.

Weiss watched intently as the cement slowly enveloped the submarine, inch by inch. He imagined the years stretching ahead, the vessel lying dormant beneath the layers of cement and water, a hidden threat waiting to resurface. The thought gave him a grim sense of satisfaction; they were ensuring the future of the Reich, even in defeat.

Once the cement had been poured to the required depth, the workers switched tasks, preparing to flood the pit. Weiss stepped back, allowing them space to work. The floodgates were opened, and water began to pour in, quickly rising to cover the cement.

Weiss turned his attention to the SS lieutenant overlooking the concentration camp laborers. "After the flooding is complete, see to it that these workers are taken care of," he said, his tone cold and detached. "We cannot afford any loose ends."

The Lieutenant glanced at the prisoners, a sneer on his face, quickly replaced by obedience. "Understood, Admiral." The water churned and bubbled as it filled the pit, gradually settling into a calm, opaque surface. No one would suspect what lay beneath—the ultimate secret, concealed from the world.

Weiss took one last look at the water-filled pit, the final resting place of U-boat 420. With a deep breath, he turned and walked away, confident that their secret would remain buried until the time was right.

As he turned to leave the U-boat bunkers, he heard the SS lieutenant issue orders to have the Jewish prisoners line up against one of the thick walls followed by deafening machine gun fire.

CHAPTER 4

Dr. Lena Lawrence surfaced from the cold waters of the fjord, her SCUBA gear glistening with droplets. She pushed her mask up onto her forehead and glanced around. The submerged entrance to the U-boat bunker had been a challenging dive, but the relics she found made it worthwhile. She swam to the edge of the dock where Alex Sousa waited, his notebook in hand.

"Find anything interesting, Lena?" Alex asked with a teasing grin, using her playful nickname.

Lena hoisted herself up onto the dock, dripping wet. "You bet. Look at these," she said, handing him a small, waterproof container filled with artifacts. "Some Nazi insignias, a few personal items. It's like a time capsule down there."

Alex examined the items with keen interest. "These are incredible. They must have belonged to the soldiers stationed here. Each piece tells a story."

Lena began to peel off her wetsuit, still catching her breath. "It's eerie, knowing what went on in these bunkers. There's a sense of history that's almost palpable."

Before Alex could respond, the ground beneath them trembled. A low rumble grew into a deafening roar as the earth shook violently. Lena and Alex struggled to maintain their balance, clutching the dock's railings.

"Earthquake!" Alex shouted over the noise, his eyes wide with alarm.

The tremors intensified, sending ripples across the water. Cracks began to form in the concrete structures around them, and the sound of breaking glass and crumbling masonry filled the air.

Alex grabbed Lena's arm, pulling her towards safer ground. "We need to get out of here, now!"

They stumbled away from the dock, the violent shaking making every step a struggle. Behind them, the water churned wildly, and a section of the bunker's wall collapsed into the fjord with a massive splash.

As they reached a clearing, the shaking gradually subsided, leaving behind a scene of devastation. Lena and Alex paused to catch their breath, looking back at the ruined bunker.

"That was intense," Lena panted. "I've never experienced anything like it."

"Me either. Are you okay?" Alex replied looking back at the U-boat bunkers.

"Do you think the bunkers are damaged?" Lena asked

"I doubt anything happened to the U-boat bunkers. Albert Speer used tons of reinforced concrete to withstand direct bomb impacts," Alex replied, trying to reassure her.

Despite his words, Lena couldn't shake off her anxiety. "We should check it out just to be sure," she insisted. The two approached one of the bunkers cautiously. The concrete structure loomed ahead, imposing and seemingly impenetrable. Lena ran her hand along the rough surface, looking for any signs of damage.

"See," Alex said, gesturing towards the bunker walls. "Even with an earthquake of this huge magnitude, not even cracks have penetrated the structure."

Lena peered closely at the walls, her fingers tracing the edges. "You're right," she admitted, a hint of relief in her voice. "It looks like the reinforced concrete held up."

Alex nodded, his confidence growing. "Speer's designs were incredibly robust. These bunkers were built to last, to survive anything." They continued their inspection, walking around the perimeter of the bunker. As they turned a corner, Lena paused, her eyes narrowing as she noticed something unusual.

"Alex, come here," Lena called out, pointing to a section of water just outside one of the bunkers.

Alex hurried over, his curiosity piqued. "What is it?"

Lena knelt down, brushing away debris in the water. "This might be nothing, but it's worth investigating. If the earthquake caused a shift in the ground, it could lead to problems later on. Look at the air bubbles rising. I think the earth might have separated somewhat down below. Help me put my diving gear back on. I want to go back down as soon as possible."

"Wait a minute," Alex interjected. "I know you can't wait to go back down there, but we need to monitor you since we don't know what's down there. What if some discarded rebar has shifted and you get tangled up? No, wait for me to suit up and I will join you."

Lena hesitated but then nodded, appreciating Alex's caution. "Alright, you're right. Let's suit up together."

As they headed back to the research center, the weight of their discovery pressed heavily on them. The earthquake might not have caused immediate visible damage, but the hidden threats beneath the surface were a reminder of the precariousness of their situation.

Inside the research center, there was a buzz of activity. Alina and others were gathered around seismic monitoring equipment and data collection tools. As Alina saw them, she quickly yelled out, "That was an 8.2 earthquake."

"We need to keep a close watch on these bunkers and the surrounding area," Lena instructed. "If there's even a slight shift, we need to know about it. Dr. Sousa and I are going back down in one of the bunkers to check it out."

Lena's eyes widened with concern. "An 8.2? That's massive. I want you to monitor our dive. We will communicate as we descend."

"Rodger, that," a playful Alina responds.

Lena and Alex smile and make their way to the bunker quickly preparing their diving gear. The urgency of the situation fueled their determination. They double-checked their equipment and ensured their communication devices were working perfectly.

As they made their way back to the water's edge, Lena took a deep breath, steeling herself for what lay ahead. "Ready, Alex?"

"Ready," he confirmed, adjusting his mask. "Let's find out what's going on down there."

They entered the water together, the cold immediately enveloping them. Descending slowly, Lena led the way, her flashlight cutting through the murky depths. The sight of air bubbles rising from the fissure below confirmed her suspicions. The earthquake had indeed disturbed what appeared to be a cement tomb.

Alex swam beside her, his eyes scanning the surroundings for any signs of danger. They reached the fissure, and Lena pointed her light into the dark crevice. The once solid ground now showed signs of separation, small cracks spiderwebbing out from the main fissure.

"We need to document this," Alex said through their communication link. "And we have to be quick. This area isn't stable yet."

Lena nodded, pulling out her underwater camera. She snapped several photos, capturing the extent of the damage. As she did, she noticed something glinting within the crack—something metallic.

"Alex, look at this," she said, pointing to the object. "It's part of the structure. The quake must have exposed it."

They carefully examined the area, avoiding any loose debris. The metallic object appeared to be part of the U-boat's outer shell, now partially visible due to the shifting earth.

"We've got what we need," Lena said, securing the camera. "Let's head back up and analyze this data."

As they ascended, Lena couldn't help but feel a sense of foreboding. The earthquake had revealed a glimpse of what lay beneath, but it also raised questions about what else might be unearthed if the fissure widened further.

Breaking the surface, they were met with concerned faces. Alina rushed to help them out of the water. "What did you find?"

Lena handed her the camera. "The earthquake caused a fissure. Part of what appears to be a U-boat's shell is exposed. We need to analyze these images and monitor the area closely."

Alina nodded, her face serious. "A U-boat. Wow! We'll get started right away."

As they stripped off their gear, Lena turned to Alex. "This is just the beginning. We need to be prepared for whatever else might come."

Alex agreed, his expression resolute. "We'll face it together. Whatever it takes."

With a cup of coffee each, the two watch Alina download the photos taken by Lena. Magnified, the outer shell appears to definitely be that of a World War II German submarine.

"Alex, we need to go back down there. This could be a huge discovery."

"I'm right behind you."

CHAPTER 5

Lena adjusted her dive mask and took a deep breath, the cold water pressing in on all sides as she descended. Beside her, Alex moved with deliberate strokes, his eyes scanning the underwater landscape. They followed the rising air bubbles from the fissure they had discovered the previous day. Looming ahead was a dark, jagged line in the seabed that hinted at the secrets it concealed. Alex turns on his underwater flashlight and Lena does the same.

The two divers reached the cracked concrete tomb of U-boat 420. The structure was massive, its once-impenetrable shell now marred by the earthquake's violent force. Lena swam closer, her flashlight beam cutting through the murky water to illuminate the damage.

Alex signaled to Lena, pointing to a section where the concrete slab had split wide enough to reveal the edges of what lay beneath. Despite their proximity, the contents of the tomb remained obscured in darkness, the visibility limited by sediment stirred up by the recent tremors.

Lena's heart pounded with a mixture of excitement and trepidation. She pressed her faceplate closer, trying to peer into the void. Alex joined her, their beams of light intersecting as they sought to uncover the mystery hidden within.

But the tomb's interior remained elusive. The fissure, though significant, was not wide enough to provide a clear view. Lena gestured to Alex, indicating that they should surface and regroup. He nodded in agreement, and they slowly ascended, their thoughts racing faster than their bubbles.

Breaking the surface, they removed their masks, gasping for breath in the crisp air. Alex turned to Lena, his expression a mix of frustration and determination.

"I couldn't see anything definitive," Alex admitted, pulling off his fins and setting them on the U-boat bunker dock. "We need more light and probably a way to clear some of that sediment."

Lena nodded, wringing the water from her hair. "Agreed. But there's something there, Alex. I can feel it."

Alex rubbed his chin, deep in thought. "I have a hunch this has something to do with a special project, but I need to do some more research. Something about this tomb feels... significant. I'll dig into the archives tonight, see if I can find any references to a hidden U-boat or a secret project conducted here."

Lena smiled, appreciating Alex's thoroughness. "While you do that, I'll figure out what equipment we need. More powerful lights, maybe some underwater cameras, and a way to clear the debris. Also, maybe some type of hydraulic device to help us shift the concrete. We should be prepared for anything."

As they secured their gear and headed back to the shore, Lena's mind buzzed with the possibilities. The cracked concrete tomb had piqued their curiosity, but it was clear they had only scratched the surface of its secrets. The real discovery awaited them, hidden in the darkness below.

That night, while Alex pored over old documents and naval records, Lena made a list of the equipment they would need for their next dive. She contacted suppliers, arranged for rentals, and ensured that everything would be ready for their return to the site the following day.

Lena looked at her watch and saw that it was almost midnight. She disrobed and climbed into bed lying there, thinking about tomorrow's dive. Exhausted, Lena finally succumbed to sleep, but her rest was far from peaceful.

In the depths of her slumber, she was transported to a different time, a different place. The dream began abruptly; she found herself jostled and shaken awake in a dark, cramped cattle car. The air was thick with fear and desperation, the cries of men, women, and children surrounding her. The stench of sweat, urine, and fear choked her, making it hard to breathe. Dead bodies were on the floor.

Lena's eyes darted around, trying to make sense of her surroundings. The realization hit her like a blow—she was among Jewish prisoners being transported during the Holocaust. Panic gripped her as the train came to a screeching halt. The only door on the side of the car was yanked open, and harsh commands in German echoed through the night.

"Raus! Schnell, Schnell!" SS personnel barked, their voices filled with cruelty.

People stumbled out of the car, some too weak to move quickly enough. Those who lagged were clubbed viciously, the sounds of blows and cries merging into a horrifying symphony. Lena's heart raced as she struggled to keep up with the crowd, her breath coming in short, terrified gasps. Thick, acrid smoke filled the air, burning her throat and making her eyes water.

She knew what was happening. The dread, the hopelessness, it all felt crushingly real. Her mind screamed to wake up, to escape this nightmare, but her body was rooted in the horror of the moment.

Suddenly, she was shoved roughly, the impact jolting her awake. Lena sat up in bed, drenched in cold sweat, her heart pounding as if it would burst from her chest. She took several deep breaths, trying to calm herself, the echoes of the nightmare slowly fading.

Shaking, she wiped the sweat from her brow and glanced at the clock. It was just past 3 a.m. Lena lay back down, the adrenaline still coursing through her veins, making it impossible to fall back asleep.

**

As dawn broke over the fjord, Lena felt a renewed sense of purpose mixed with an underlying unease. The nightmare had shaken her, but it also strengthened her resolve. She knew that whatever they found beneath the cracked tomb could hold the key to understanding a dark chapter of history—and she was determined to uncover it.

Lena made her way to the dining room area of the research facility, the aroma of freshly brewed coffee mingling with the scent of scrambled eggs and toast. Alex was already there, hunched over a stack of old documents and naval records, a steaming mug of coffee by his side.

"Morning, Alex," Lena greeted, grabbing a plate and joining him at the table.

"Morning, Lena," Alex replied, looking up from his papers. "How'd you sleep?"

Lena hesitated, then decided to share the nightmare that had disturbed her so deeply. "Not well, actually. I had a horrendous nightmare. I was in a cattle car with other Jewish prisoners, men, women, and children. The train stopped, and the SS forced us out with shouts and blows. The stench and smoke were suffocating. It felt so real."

Alex's expression grew serious. "That sounds awful, Lena. It's no wonder you're shaken. The mind can conjure up some terrifying images, especially when we're dealing with such intense subject matter. Being in this place, with all its history and associations, could have added to the vividness of your dream."

Lena nodded, taking a sip of her coffee. "I think it was triggered by everything we're uncovering. The horrors of that time... it just felt like I was living through it."

Alex reached across the table and squeezed her hand. "You're not alone in this. We're in this together, and we'll face whatever we find, side by side."

Lena smiled gratefully, then gestured to the documents in front of him. "Did you find anything in your research?"

Alex leaned back in his chair, gathering his thoughts. "Yes, actually. Towards the end of the war, Hitler became increasingly delusional. His obsession with creating wonder weapons, or 'Wunderwaffe,' as he called them, reached new heights of insanity. He believed that these superweapons would turn the tide of the war in Germany's favor, despite the overwhelming evidence to the contrary."

"There were countless projects, each more ambitious and outlandish than the last. Some were laughably impractical, like the giant sun gun that was supposed to harness the power of the sun to burn enemy cities to ashes. Others, however, advanced significantly and posed real threats."

"For instance, there was the V-2 rocket, the world's first long-range guided ballistic missile, which was responsible for thousands of deaths in London and Antwerp. Then there was the Horten Ho 229, a jet-powered flying wing that could have changed aerial warfare if it had been produced in sufficient numbers."

"The Nazis also experimented with chemical and biological weapons, though fortunately, these projects never came to full fruition. Another frightening project was the development of nuclear technology. While they never succeeded in creating a functional atomic bomb, the very fact that they were working on such a weapon is chilling."

"One of the more secretive and sinister projects was the 'Erneuerung' or 'Renewal' project. It involved the creation of a futuristic U-boat, the U-boat 420, which was equipped with cryonics technology. The idea was to place its crew in suspended animation, allowing them to reawaken in the future and revive the Nazi regime."

"This project was incredibly advanced for its time and required a significant amount of resources and technological expertise. The fact that they were willing to invest so much in such a speculative and long-term plan speaks volumes about the state of desperation and delusion that Hitler and his inner circle were in during the final days of the Third Reich."

Lena's eyes widened. "Cryonics? Like freezing people to preserve them for the future?"

"Exactly," Alex confirmed. "According to the documents, this U-boat was designed to resurface at a later date, ensuring the continuation of the Third Reich. There's a hidden reference indicating that this U-boat, U-boat 420, was hidden in a secret location—right where we are currently conducting our research."

Lena's pulse quickened. "Do you think the cracked concrete tomb we found could be related to this U-boat?"

Alex nodded slowly. "It's highly possible. The earthquake may have exposed a part of this secret project. If that's the case, we might be standing on the brink of uncovering one of the most significant finds in World War II history."

The gravity of their discovery settled over them, a mixture of excitement and dread. Lena took a deep breath, her resolve hardening. "We need to be ready for whatever we find down there. Let's make sure we have all the equipment we need for the next dive."

Alex agreed, his determination matching hers. Together, they would face the unknown, prepared to reveal the secrets buried beneath the concrete tomb.

CHAPTER 6

The morning sun cast a golden glow over the fjord as Lena and Alex loaded their small dive boat with the necessary equipment. The air was filled with a sense of anticipation, mixed with the salty tang of the sea. Lena checked the list one last time, ensuring they had everything they needed: powerful lights, underwater cameras, debris-clearing tools, and the hydraulic device they hoped would shift the concrete slab.

"Looks like we're ready to go," Alex said, hefting a heavy coil of rope onto the deck. He glanced at Lena with a playful smile. "Hope you got enough sleep after that nightmare."

Lena chuckled, her eyes sparkling despite the lingering tension from her dream. "I did, and thanks to a strong cup of coffee this morning I'm rearing to go. Besides, having you around makes it easier to shake off the bad dreams."

Alex raised an eyebrow, a mischievous grin spreading across his face. “Is that so? Well, I’m glad to be of service.”

As they finished loading the equipment, Lena couldn’t help but tease Alex back. “Just make sure you don’t get too distracted down there. We have a lot of work to do.”

“Distracted? Me?” Alex feigned innocence, causing Lena to laugh. “I’ll try to stay focused, but with such good company, it’s going to be a challenge.”

They both laughed, the lighthearted banter easing the tension and fueling their excitement for the dive ahead. Once everything was secured, they donned their dive suits, the snug neoprene fabric clinging to their bodies as they prepared for the descent.

“Ready?” Lena asked, adjusting her mask.

“Always,” Alex replied, his eyes meeting hers with a look of determination and a hint of flirtation.

They slipped into the water, the coolness enveloping them as they descended into the depths. The world above faded away, replaced by the serene, otherworldly landscape of the underwater realm. They swam towards the fissure in the concrete tomb. Their powerful lights cutting through the dim water as they focused on the rising air bubbles. Alex carried the hydraulic device similar to what firefighters use to free individuals from vehicles.

The crack in the concrete loomed ahead, larger and more imposing than they remembered. Lena and Alex worked in tandem, setting up the hydraulic device and positioning it carefully against the slab. The machine whirred to life, its mechanical arms slowly prying at the edges of the crack.

After what felt like an eternity of effort, the slab began to shift. The hydraulic tool strained against the weight, but finally, with a groan of protest, the concrete slab moved just enough to reveal what lay beneath.

There it was, unmistakable and awe-inspiring—the sleek, dark silhouette of a U-boat, its lines cutting through the water like a ghost from the past. Lena's heart raced with excitement, her earlier fear and tension replaced by a surge of adrenaline.

She glanced at Alex, who gave her an enthusiastic thumbs-up. They both knew the significance of their discovery. They had uncovered a piece of history that had been hidden for decades, a relic of a time filled with dark secrets and unimaginable ambition.

With their initial exploration complete, Lena signaled to Alex, and they began their ascent. Breaking the surface, they removed their masks, gasping for breath and grinning from ear to ear.

"We did it, Lena," Alex said, his voice filled with awe. "We actually found it."

Lena nodded, her mind racing with possibilities. "This is just the beginning. We need to document everything and plan our next steps carefully."

As they secured their gear and prepared to head back to the research facility, Lena's curiosity couldn't be contained. "Alex, why do you think the Nazis decided to bury this U-boat at the mouth of one of the U-boat bunkers, just out of the reach of diving from the shore?"

Alex pondered for a moment, his brow furrowing in thought. "It's a good question. From what I've read, the Nazis were masters of deception and misdirection. They likely chose this location for several reasons. First, it was close enough to their existing infrastructure to facilitate construction and maintenance but far enough from prying eyes and potential sabotage."

He continued, "Secondly, the mouth of the fjord is a natural choke point, making it an excellent strategic location. By placing the U-boat here, they could ensure it remained hidden and protected, while still being able to monitor and control access to the fjord. Plus, the depth and the harsh conditions would deter casual divers or treasure hunters. Only someone with serious determination and the right equipment, like us, would be able to find it."

Lena nodded, considering his words. "That makes sense. They wanted to ensure it stayed hidden until the right moment, whenever that might have been."

"Exactly," Alex agreed. "And now it's up to us to uncover the rest of its secrets. This is a major find, Lena. We need to be meticulous in our approach to document everything."

The gravity of their discovery settled over them, a mixture of excitement and dread. Lena took a deep breath, her resolve hardening. "We need to be ready for whatever we find down there. Let's make sure we have all the equipment we need for the next dive."

Alex agreed, his determination matching hers. He looked at her with a warm smile. "I think you and I need to celebrate. How about dinner on me tonight?"

Lena's eyes sparkled with appreciation and a hint of something more. "I'd love that. Maybe with a little alcohol in me, I'll sleep like a baby."

Alex chuckled, the tension of the day easing with their playful banter. "Sounds like a plan. Let's make it a night to remember."

Lena nodded, her heart lifting at the prospect. Despite the daunting task ahead, she felt a growing connection with Alex, their shared passion for discovery intertwining with a burgeoning friendship—and perhaps something deeper.

CHAPTER 7

The evening air was crisp and filled with the scent of the sea as Alex and Lena made their way to a quaint restaurant near the research facility. The anticipation of their discovery hung in the air, but for now, they allowed themselves a moment of respite.

They found a cozy corner table and ordered a bottle of wine to accompany their meal. The soft glow of candlelight created an intimate atmosphere, making it easy for them to relax and enjoy each other's company.

"To new discoveries," Alex said, raising his glass.

"To new discoveries," Lena echoed, clinking her glass against his.

As they sipped their wine, the conversation flowed easily, shifting from their work to more personal topics.

"So, Lena, what brought you into the world of marine biology and historical research?" Alex asked, genuinely curious.

Lena smiled, her eyes reflecting the candlelight. "I grew up near the ocean, always fascinated by its mysteries. My father was a historian, and he used to tell me stories about sunken ships and lost treasures. I guess it was only natural for me to combine both interests."

Alex nodded, intrigued. "That's a unique blend. My interest in history started with my grandfather's stories about World War II. He was a soldier, and his tales always had a way of captivating my imagination."

They continued to share stories, revealing bits of their pasts that had shaped who they were. With each glass of wine, the barriers between them lowered, and the conversation grew more personal.

Lena laughed softly, her cheeks flushed from the wine. "I have to admit, I haven't felt this relaxed in a long time."

Alex leaned in, his eyes locked on hers. "I'm glad to hear that. You deserve a break after everything we've been through."

As the evening wore on, they decided to call it a night. Alex stood and offered his arm to Lena, who accepted with a smile. They walked back to the research center, their steps slow and unhurried, savoring the quiet of the night.

"Thanks for tonight, Alex. I really needed this," Lena said, leaning into him slightly.

"I'm happy you enjoyed it," Alex replied, his voice low and warm. "But the night's not over yet."

They reached Lena's room, and Alex paused, his hand lingering on her arm. "I had a great time tonight, Lena."

"So did I," she replied, her gaze dropping to his lips and then back to his eyes.

Alex took a step closer, the tension between them palpable. "Maybe we should do this more often."

"Maybe we should," Lena whispered, her breath hitching as Alex closed the distance.

Without another word, he leaned in and kissed her softly, testing the waters. When Lena responded, wrapping her arms around his neck, the kiss deepened, becoming more passionate.

They stumbled into Lena's room, the door closing behind them. Clothes were discarded hastily as they made their way to the bed, the culmination of their shared excitement and mutual attraction. They spent the night exploring each other, solidifying a bond that would be crucial for the challenges ahead.

**

The next morning, the sun peeked through the curtains, casting a warm glow over the room. Lena woke up first, her mind still fuzzy from the wine and the night's events. She glanced over at Alex, who was still asleep, and a smile played on her lips. The connection they had felt was undeniable, but she couldn't help but think about the implications for their work.

As Lena quietly got out of bed and dressed, she reflected on their discovery of the U-boat. The excitement was still fresh, and she knew they had to move quickly to document and secure the site. She gently shook Alex awake.

"Hey, rise and shine. We've got a U-boat waiting for us," she said, her voice soft but firm.

Alex groaned and opened his eyes, smiling when he saw Lena. "Morning already? I could get used to waking up like this," he said, sitting up and stretching.

They shared a quick breakfast and discussed their plan for the day. They needed to gather more equipment and make sure they were prepared for a thorough exploration of the U-boat. Lena suggested they contact a colleague who specialized in World War II artifacts for advice on how to proceed without damaging the site.

"I agree, but I think, first we should see if we can gather any photos of the site down below and possibly see if I can stretch my arm with a camera into the narrow slot we made yesterday on the slab. After we gather some pictures, we can surface and then decide what our next course of action should be. What do you think?" Alex stated.

Lena nodded, "That sounds like a solid plan. If we can get clear images, it will help us assess the condition of the U-boat without causing any unnecessary damage. Plus, having visual documentation will be crucial when we bring in our colleague and eventually notify the authorities."

They geared up and headed out to the dive site, the excitement of the previous day still fresh in their minds. As they descended, Alex maneuvered himself to the narrow slot they had created in the concrete slab. With careful precision, he extended his arm, camera in hand, and began snapping photos. The dim light from their dive torches illuminated the haunting interior of the U-boat, revealing more details with each click.

Satisfied with their initial photographic survey, they surfaced and reviewed the images. The pictures showed a remarkably well-preserved submarine interior, with personal items and equipment eerily untouched by time. On the coning tower were the numbers 420.

Back at the research center, Lena and Alex pored over the photos. "We need an expert's opinion on this," Lena said, her voice serious. "This isn't just a historical find; it looks like there could be significant artifacts and possibly even sensitive information on board."

Alex nodded in agreement. "Let's contact Dr. Müller. His expertise in World War II German naval history will be invaluable. And we should start drafting a report for the U.S. State Department. They can coordinate with the Norwegian authorities so that a joint operation can take place. This discovery is too important to handle on our own."

Dr. Hans Müller was a renowned historian with a specialization in naval warfare during World War II. Having published numerous books and papers on the subject, he was considered one of the leading experts in his field. His work often took him to historical sites around the world, and he had a reputation for being thorough and meticulous in his research. Lena and Alex had met him at an international maritime conference a few years back and had stayed in touch ever since, occasionally consulting him on complex historical matters.

They spent the next few hours meticulously documenting their findings and preparing their correspondence. Lena reached out to Dr. Müller, explaining their discovery and the need for his expertise.

"Dr. Müller, this is Dr. Lena Lawrence. Dr. Alex Sousa and I have made an incredible discovery—an intact World War II U-boat encased in a concrete tomb just outside one of the U-boat bunkers in Burgen, Norway. We need your expertise to properly assess and handle this find. Can you assist us?"

Dr. Müller's voice crackled over the phone. "Lena, this sounds extraordinary! There were rumors that the Nazis created a super-sub and hid it. You two may have found it. I'll arrange to come out immediately. In the meantime, document everything you can without disturbing the site. We must preserve its integrity. I will get the first flight out."

Meanwhile, Alex began drafting the necessary notifications to the U.S. State Department. He detailed their discovery, emphasizing the historical significance and the need for a coordinated effort with the Norwegian authorities. The State Department would be able to facilitate the international collaboration needed to explore and preserve the U-boat.

As the day drew to a close, they knew their discovery was just the beginning of a much larger journey. The U-boat held secrets that could reshape historical narratives, and it was up to them to ensure those secrets were uncovered and preserved with the utmost care and respect. They felt a sense of responsibility and anticipation for what lay ahead, knowing they were on the brink of revealing a piece of history long thought lost to the depths of the sea.

Both returned to Alex's room and laid on the bed next to each other. "I guess all we can do is wait," Lena said, placing her head on Alex's chest.

CHAPTER 8

The two awoke from a short nap and decided to check the mess hall of the research facility for lunch. The mess hall was bustling with activity as researchers and staff chatted over their meals. Alina, already in the dining area, bounced up to the two as they entered.

"Dr. Lena, have you checked your emails? I didn't want to disturb you when it came in, but it is from the State Department," Alina said, her voice tinged with excitement and urgency.

Lena wiped some mayonnaise from her face and quickly grabbed her cellphone. She found the email Alina was referring to and read it aloud.

"Dr. Lena Lawrence, this email acknowledges you and Dr. Alex Sousa's remarkable find in Bergen. We are currently in talks with the Norwegian government. We are working out the logistics of our two governments working together as well as making a decision on whether Germany must be brought in.

At this time, we request that NO further exploration of the U-boat is conducted until all parties are in agreement. In addition, we are immediately sending a small detachment of Army personnel as well as Naval SEAL Commander Mark Davis, who will be in charge of security of the area. Other emails will follow as necessary."

"Who sent it?" Alex asked, leaning in to get a closer look at Lena's phone.

Lena checked the sender's details. "A Jennifer Connelly, Assistant Secretary of State."

"Never heard of her," Alex interjected. "Her email pretty much shuts us down for now. Do you know when Dr. Müller will arrive? At least we can do our due diligence about what might be down there."

Lena looked at Alina, who nodded. "Dr. Müller sent an email to the research center saying he should arrive early tomorrow morning."

"Well, like I said. Hurry up and wait," Alex said with a sigh.

They finished their lunch in contemplative silence, the weight of the email's implications sinking in. The excitement of their discovery was now tempered by the realization of the bureaucratic and international hurdles they had to navigate.

After lunch, Lena and Alex headed back to their lab to ensure all their findings and documentation were in order. They meticulously organized their photos, notes, and initial analyses, preparing for Dr. Müller's arrival and the potential influx of military personnel.

As evening approached, the research facility's normally quiet atmosphere was abuzz with rumors and speculations about the U-boat and the imminent arrival of government officials and security forces. Lena couldn't help but feel a mix of pride and anxiety. Their discovery was monumental, but it also brought with it a level of scrutiny and control that could complicate their work.

Back in her office, Lena drafted an email to Dr. Müller, updating him on the latest developments and emphasizing the urgency of his expertise. She also reached out to a few trusted colleagues for additional support, anticipating that the coming days would be challenging.

That night, as Lena and Alex sat on the deck overlooking the ocean, they talked about their hopes and concerns. The U-boat was more than just an archaeological find; it was a piece of history that needed to be handled with the utmost care and respect.

"We've done everything we can for now," Lena said, staring out at the darkening horizon. "Tomorrow, with Dr. Müller here and the State Department's team arriving, we'll have a clearer path forward."

Alex nodded. "Let's get some rest. We're going to need it."

As they headed back to Alex's quarters, the weight of the day's events settled over them. The magnitude of their discovery loomed large in their minds, the anticipation of what was to come intertwining with the gravity of the historical implications. They knew the coming days would be pivotal, not just for their research, but for the historical significance of what they had uncovered.

After an exciting, intimate reunion, the two lay next to each other in a tender embrace. Alex ran his fingers gently through Lena's hair, the simple gesture soothing her lingering anxieties.

"That feels nice," she murmured, her eyes half-closed in contentment.

Alex hesitated, his hand pausing momentarily before he continued. "I didn't tell you the other day when you told me about your nightmare, the one where you found yourself on a transport to one of the death camps."

Lena turned to face him, curiosity and concern in her eyes. "What is it, Alex?"

He removed his hand from her head and moved it to her bare shoulder, drawing small circles with his thumb. "My great aunt and uncle were Jews. In 1944, when most Germans knew the war was not going well, they were rounded up with others in their village and transported to Auschwitz."

"My great grandparents tried to locate them after the war, hoping that maybe they had survived the Holocaust. That's when they discovered that both were gassed as soon as the transport train arrived."

Lena's breath caught, and she placed her hand over his, squeezing gently. "I'm so sorry, Alex. I had no idea."

He nodded, his gaze distant as he continued. "It's something my family doesn't talk about much, but it's always there, a shadow over our history. Finding this U-boat, uncovering these secrets—it's not just about the past. It's personal. It's a chance to honor them, to bring to light stories that were buried in the darkness."

Lena leaned in, resting her forehead against his. "We'll do this right, Alex. For them, for everyone who suffered. We'll make sure their stories are told."

They lay in silence for a while, the weight of their conversation mingling with the exhaustion of the day. The night was a tapestry of unspoken promises and shared resolve, the bond between them growing stronger with each passing moment.

CHAPTER 9

As the first light of dawn began to creep into the room, Lena and Alex lay in a tranquil embrace, the morning's gentle glow casting a soft light on their intertwined bodies. The stillness of the early hour was a stark contrast to the whirlwind of events that had unfolded, but the tranquility brought clarity and determination.

Lena stirred first, feeling the warmth of Alex's arm around her. She turned slightly to see his peaceful face, and for a moment, she allowed herself to bask in the simplicity of the moment. But reality soon intruded, and she knew they had a long day ahead.

"Time to get up," she whispered, her voice gentle but firm. Alex groaned in response, reluctant to leave the comfort of their cocoon.

"Five more minutes?" he mumbled, eyes still closed.

Lena chuckled softly, planting a light kiss on his forehead. "We've got a lot to do today. Dr. Müller will be arriving soon, and we need to be ready."

Alex opened his eyes, the gravity of their situation settling back in. "You're right. Let's get moving."

They disentangled themselves and began to get take a shower which led to more lovemaking. Once finished they dressed, the routine actions grounding them as they prepared for the challenges ahead. The research facility was starting to come alive with activity as they made their way to the lab.

Over a quick breakfast, they reviewed their plans. Lena updated Alex on the latest emails and preparations for Dr. Müller's arrival. The research center had been abuzz with excitement and speculation since the news of their discovery spread, and they knew today would be pivotal.

"We need to be prepared for the State Department's team as well," Lena said, checking her notes. "Commander Mark Davis is expected to arrive with his team to secure the site. We'll need to coordinate with him to ensure everything goes smoothly."

Alex nodded, his mind already racing with the logistics. "And we should have all our documentation and findings ready for Dr. Müller. His expertise will be crucial in the next steps. We need to make sure we're fully briefed and can give him all the information he needs."

As they finished their breakfast, the intercom crackled to life, announcing the arrival of Dr. Müller's flight. Lena and Alex exchanged a look, a mix of anticipation and nervous energy coursing through them.

"Here we go," Alex said, standing up and gathering his things. "Let's make history."

They headed to the research center's main entrance to greet Dr. Müller. The historian emerged from the vehicle, his keen eyes taking in the facility and the palpable excitement in the air. Bald and heavy set in his early eighties, he still was as sharp as a tack and nimble on his feet. He greeted Lena and Alex with a firm handshake and a warm smile.

"Lena, Alex, it's good to see you both," Dr. Müller said, his voice resonating with authority and enthusiasm. "I've read your preliminary reports, and I must say, this discovery is extraordinary."

"Thank you, Dr. Müller. We're honored to have you here," Lena replied, her respect for the historian evident.

He turned and saw his assistant, a Tom Chambers, struggling with a large, oversized crate containing Dr. Muller's research. "Are you going to make it, Tom," he asked. Alex assisted Tom and the four made it to dining area so that Muller and his assistant could get some refreshments after a long flight.

They then escorted Dr. Müller to the lab, where they had laid out all their findings. After placing on a pair of reading glasses he began to examine the photos and notes; his expression grew more intense and focused.

"This is remarkable," he murmured, flipping through the images of the U-boat's exterior. "The preservation is astounding, and the historical implications… We have a lot of work ahead of us."

They spent the next few hours in deep discussion, Dr. Müller providing insights and guidance on how to proceed as he went back and forth with his reference books and material. His extensive knowledge of World War II naval history proved invaluable, and Lena and Alex felt a renewed sense of purpose and clarity.

Dr. Müller leaned over the table, his fingers tracing the outline of the U-boat in the photographs. "This, my friends, is no ordinary submarine," he began, his voice taking on a grave tone. "Towards the end of the war, as Hitler's grip on Europe was slipping, he and his inner circle became obsessed with creating a doomsday weapon—something that could strike fear into the hearts of their enemies long after the Third Reich had fallen."

Alex and Lena exchanged a glance, their interest piqued. "A doomsday weapon?" Alex asked.

"Yes," Dr. Müller continued. "Hitler believed that if the Reich were to fall, his U-boat could rise again from the ashes. He envisioned a super submarine, a vessel so advanced and terrifying that its mere existence would inspire modern-day Nazis to resurrect a Fourth Reich. This U-boat was meant to be a symbol of that enduring power."

"So, you believe as Lena and I do, that this might be the submarine code named Etneuerung?" Alex asked.

Dr. Mueller removed his glasses and rubbed his eyes. "Exactly. I believe what we have here is Hitler's state-of-the-art Super Submarine."

Lena leaned in closer, captivated by Dr. Müller's narrative. "What made this submarine so special?" she asked.

Dr. Müller sighed, flipping through his notes. "It was designed to be larger and more technologically advanced than any other submarine of its time. It was equipped with state-of-the-art weaponry, including long-range missiles and advanced torpedoes. But it wasn't just a weapon of war—it was a vessel of terror. Hitler intended it to carry out surprise attacks, sinking enemy ships and spreading fear across the seas. The primary targets being Russian, Great Britain, and the United States."

He paused, his eyes scanning the room. "But the true horror lay in its potential to carry nuclear or biological weapons. Hitler's scientists were working on these technologies, and while they never fully succeeded, the plans for this submarine included the capability to launch such devastating attacks."

Lena shivered, the enormity of their discovery sinking in. "So, this U-boat could have been a game-changer if it had been fully operational?"

"Indeed," Dr. Müller replied. "But it was more than just a weapon. It was meant to be a beacon for future generations of Nazis, a symbol of Hitler's unyielding vision. He believed that if the world were reminded of the power of the Third Reich, it would inspire a resurgence of his ideology."

Alex frowned, contemplating the implications. "Do you think there are still people out there who would be inspired by this? People who would try to bring back the Fourth Reich?"

Dr. Müller nodded slowly. "Unfortunately, there are always those who cling to such hateful ideologies. That's why it's crucial that we handle this discovery with the utmost care. The information we uncover here must be used to educate and prevent, not to incite further hatred."

Lena took a deep breath, her resolve hardening. "We have a responsibility to ensure that this history relic is properly documented and understood. We can't let it fall into the wrong hands."

"Precisely," Dr. Müller agreed. "That's why we need to proceed cautiously. The State Department's involvement is necessary to secure the site and ensure that this information is disseminated responsibly. We can't afford to make any mistakes."

They spent the rest of the afternoon meticulously documenting their findings, Dr. Müller's expertise guiding their every step. The historian's detailed explanations and insights into Hitler's twisted vision provided a sobering context to their work, underscoring the importance of their mission.

As the sun set, casting long shadows across the research facility, Lena and Alex felt a renewed sense of purpose. They were not just uncovering history; they were safeguarding the future. The days ahead would be challenging, filled with bureaucratic obstacles and the heavy burden of history, but they were ready to face them together, driven by a shared commitment to uncovering the truth.

As they wrapped up their long briefing, an aide entered the lab to inform them of Commander Mark Davis's arrival. Lena and Alex exchanged another look, knowing that the next phase of their journey was about to begin.

CHAPTER 10

Together, Lena, Alex, and Dr. Mueller walked out to meet the commander, their steps in sync, their resolve unwavering. They were ready to face the challenges, bureaucratic obstacles, and the heavy burden of history. Driven by a shared purpose and a commitment to uncovering the truth, Lena and Alex knew that they were on the brink of making history.

Commander Davis was an imposing figure with short, blond hair, often styled in a military buzz cut. His sharp blue eyes, tanned skin, and sturdy build make him an authoritative presence, one that commands respect and attention whenever he enters a room.

A seasoned Navy SEAL, Commander Davis has a rich background in special operations. Having joined the Navy in his late teens, he quickly distinguished himself through his acute strategic sense and physical prowess. He has been deployed in multiple global hotspots, earning a reputation as a skilled tactician and a leader who deeply cares for the safety and well-being of his team.

"Commander Davis," Lena began, extending her hand. "We're honored to have you here."

Davis shook her hand firmly, his grip conveying both strength and reassurance. "Dr. Lawrence, Dr. Sousa, Dr. Mueller, the honor is mine. I've been briefed on your discovery, and I must say, it's extraordinary."

They led him to the lab where the findings were laid out. As they walked, Davis moved with a purposeful stride, his movements precise and efficient. He exuded a calm confidence, maintaining a level head even as they delved into the complexities of the mission.

Once inside the lab, Davis listened intently to their explanations, his sharp mind quickly absorbing the details. "This, my friend, is no ordinary submarine," Dr. Müller began, as Davis leaned over the table, examining the photos and notes with keen interest.

Davis's presence brought a renewed sense of discipline and focus. His tactical knowledge and strategic thinking became evident as he offered suggestions on securing the site and coordinating with the incoming teams. He carefully planned every move, visualizing several steps ahead, ensuring that the operation would proceed smoothly.

"Your leadership and expertise will be crucial in the days to come," Lena said, appreciating his meticulous attention to detail and the clear, concise way he communicated his plans.

Davis nodded. "We'll make sure everything is handled with the utmost care. This discovery has the potential to reshape historical narratives, and we must ensure it's done responsibly."

Throughout the discussions, Davis's empathy and moral integrity shone through. He balanced the harsh realities of their mission with a firm moral compass, ensuring that their actions would be justified and humane. In confrontational moments, he remained composed but firm, his steady gaze and calm demeanor making it clear that he was not one to be underestimated.

"So, where do we go from here?" Alex asked, his voice carrying a mix of curiosity and determination. The three of them turned to Commander Davis, awaiting his response.

Commander Davis, standing tall and exuding a quiet confidence, took a moment to assess the situation before speaking. "My immediate orders are to secure the facility and the surrounding area," he began, his voice steady and authoritative. "Our primary objective is to ensure the safety and integrity of the site. This includes setting up a perimeter to prevent unauthorized access and keeping the discovery under wraps for as long as possible."

He paused, his sharp blue eyes scanning the room, gauging their reactions. "We need to contain the news of your discovery from reaching the press. The last thing we need is a flock of media descending on the research center. This would not only disrupt our operations but could also compromise the security of the site and the artifacts."

Davis continued, his tone firm yet reassuring. "I'll be coordinating with the local authorities and our incoming team to establish a secure perimeter. We'll implement strict protocols to control access to the facility. Only authorized personnel will be allowed entry, and we'll have round-the-clock surveillance to ensure that no one gets through without proper clearance."

Alex nodded, appreciating the thoroughness of Davis's plan. "What about the Norwegian government and our contacts there?"

"We're in constant communication with them," Davis replied. "The State Department is handling the diplomatic aspects to ensure that we have their full cooperation. This will be a joint effort, and we need to make sure all parties are on the same page."

Lena stepped forward, her resolve evident. "And what about our research? How can we continue our work while maintaining such tight security?"

Davis's expression softened slightly, showing his understanding of their dedication. "Your research is critical, and we'll do everything we can to support you. We'll establish secure zones within the facility where you can continue your work without interruption. I'll ensure that you have the necessary resources and that the security measures do not hinder your progress."

He glanced at both of them, a hint of a smile playing at the corners of his mouth. "Remember, we're all in this together. Our goal is to protect this discovery and uncover its secrets responsibly. We have a unique opportunity here, and it's up to us to handle it with the care and respect it deserves." Everyone nodded in agreement.

"There's another thing we need to discuss," Commander Davis said, his voice lowering to a grave tone that immediately captured their full attention. "I think we can all agree that Hitler was deranged towards the end of the war. His obsession with creating a lasting legacy, regardless of the cost, knew no bounds."

He paused, allowing the weight of his words to settle in the room. The silence was thick with anticipation. "You three are the experts on the features of this U-boat, and with that in mind, from this point forward, we must approach your finding with the utmost caution. Safety has to be our primary concern."

Davis's sharp blue eyes scanned each of their faces, ensuring they understood the seriousness of the situation. "I wouldn't put it past Hitler to have installed booby traps both inside and outside the submarine. Hitler's madness extended to elaborate and deadly measures meant to protect his secrets. Who knows what surprises he has in store for us?"

Lena felt a chill run down her spine at the thought. The prospect of hidden traps, potentially deadly ones, added a new layer of danger to their mission. She exchanged a worried glance with Alex, who nodded slightly, sharing her apprehension.

Commander Davis continued, his voice steady but laden with caution. "We need to proceed with the assumption that the U-boat could be rigged with explosives or other traps designed to activate upon discovery or tampering. Every step we take must be calculated and precise. We'll bring in EOD specialists to assist with the initial inspection and ensure the site is safe for further exploration."

Alex swallowed hard, the tension palpable. "What kind of traps are we talking about? Explosives? Chemical weapons?"

"Potentially both," Davis replied, his expression grim. "Nazi engineers were highly creative when it came to booby traps. We could be dealing with anything from hidden mines to chemical dispersal mechanisms. We'll need to use advanced detection equipment and exercise extreme caution."

Dr. Müller, who had been listening intently, finally spoke up. "This adds a significant layer of complexity to our work, but it's essential. We must treat every inch of that submarine with suspicion until we can confirm it's safe."

Lena nodded, her resolve hardening. "Agreed. We'll need to document everything meticulously and follow protocols to the letter. The history this U-boat holds is invaluable, but not at the cost of our lives."

Commander Davis's face softened slightly, showing a flicker of empathy. "I know this is daunting, but we're in this together. We have the expertise and the resources to handle this, but we must remain vigilant. Every step we take will be deliberate and cautious. Let's proceed with the respect and care that this discovery demands."

As they stood there, united by a common purpose and a newfound sense of urgency, the room was filled with a heavy silence. The discovery of the U-boat had taken on a new, perilous dimension. They were not just uncovering history—they were navigating a potentially lethal labyrinth left behind by a madman. The path ahead was fraught with danger, but their commitment to the truth remained unwavering.

CHAPTER 11

The research facility buzzed with activity as preparations continued for the careful exploration of the U-boat. The arrival of Dr. Müller and the establishment of the security perimeter by Commander Davis had set a focused, almost intense atmosphere among the team.

Just as the morning briefing was wrapping up, the sharp ping of an incoming email notification cut through the room's ambient noise. Commander Davis pulled out his phone, his eyes narrowing as he read the urgent message.

"Attention: Commander Davis,

Please be advised that a top-secret intelligence operative from Norway, Ingrid Strand, is en route to your location. Ms. Strand possesses critical information regarding the U-boat, obtained from classified files discovered in the area where the submarine was submerged. Her arrival is of utmost importance, and her information could be vital to the ongoing operation. Ensure her safety and integrate her findings with your current research immediately.

Sincerely,

Jennifer Connelly,
Assistant Secretary of State."

Davis looked up, his expression a mix of curiosity and determination. "Looks like we're about to get some crucial intel. Dr. Ingrid Strand is on her way here, and she has top-secret information about the U-boat."

A half-hour later, the door to the briefing room opened, and a striking woman stepped in. Ingrid Strand, with her long, flowing auburn hair and piercing green eyes, commanded attention the moment she entered. She was dressed in a tailored suit that highlighted her graceful yet formidable presence. The room seemed to hold its breath as she made her way towards Davis, her gaze locked onto his.

"Commander Davis," she greeted, her voice smooth and confident. "I'm Dr. Ingrid Strand. I believe we have much to discuss."

Davis extended his hand, feeling an unexpected jolt of electricity at the touch of her firm handshake. "Welcome, Dr. Strand. I've only recently been informed of your arrival. Please, have a seat."

Davis introduced Dr. Mueller, Lena, and Alex.

After salutations ended, Ingrid sat down, her movements fluid and composed. She placed a sleek leather briefcase on the table and opened it, revealing a stack of classified documents and a laptop. "These files," she began, her tone serious, "contain information that has been kept under wraps for decades. They were discovered by Norwegian intelligence in the area where the U-boat was submerged. It's imperative that you understand the full context of what we're dealing with."

Davis nodded, his attention fully on her. "We're all ears. Please, go on."

Ingrid began to explain, her eyes flicking between the documents and the faces of those around the table. "During the war, this U-boat was part of a highly classified operation known only to a select few within the Nazi hierarchy. The files indicate that it was not just a weapon of war, but a vessel meant to transport some of Hitler's most secretive and dangerous projects. Projects that, if discovered, could have far-reaching implications even today."

She paused, allowing her words to sink in. "These projects included advanced weaponry, experimental technologies, and encrypted communications intended to be used by sleeper cells long after the fall of the Reich. The presence of these elements aboard the U-boat makes it a Pandora's box of potential threats and historical revelations."

Lena leaned forward, her curiosity piqued. “And what about the booby traps? Is there any information on those?”

Ingrid nodded, her expression grim. “Yes. The files mention a series of defensive mechanisms designed to protect the contents of the U-boat. These include explosive devices, chemical traps, and even false compartments meant to mislead anyone attempting to explore the submarine without proper knowledge. This information will be crucial in ensuring the safety of your team as you proceed.”

Commander Davis’s mind raced as he processed the gravity of Ingrid’s revelations. He glanced at her, their eyes meeting for a brief moment. Despite the seriousness of the situation, he couldn’t help but notice her striking beauty and the confident way she carried herself. But there was no time for distractions.

“Thank you, Ms. Strand,” Davis said, his voice firm and authoritative. “Your information is invaluable. We’ll need to integrate this data with our current findings and adjust our approach accordingly. We’re fortunate to have you here. Since it’s almost lunchtime, may I suggest we take a break to freshen up and then meet in the dining area in about thirty minutes? I’d love to conduct a working lunch and hear more about these booby traps in detail.”

Ingrid smiled, a hint of warmth breaking through her professional demeanor. “Please, everyone call me Ingrid. We will be working together for a long time

I feel. I'm here to help, Commander. Lunch sounds great. Let's ensure that this discovery is handled with the care and precision it deserves."

Davis returned her smile, appreciating her dedication. "Ingrid, I can show you to your room so you can freshen up. I'll knock on your door in thirty minutes and lead you to the dining section if that works for you."

"That sounds fine," Ingrid replied. "That will give me time to gather my documents and prepare a more detailed presentation for the group."

Everyone stood, the tension in the room easing slightly as they prepared to take a brief respite. As they walked out of the command center, Davis couldn't help but admire Ingrid's poise and professionalism. She moved with a grace that belied the seriousness of her mission, and her presence seemed to bring a renewed sense of focus to the team.

Davis led Ingrid down the corridor to her quarters, the hum of activity around them a constant reminder of the importance of their work. "Your room is just down here," he said, stopping in front of a door. "I hope you find everything you need. If there's anything else you require, don't hesitate to ask."

"Thank you, Commander," Ingrid said, her eyes meeting his with a sincerity that caught him off guard. "I appreciate your hospitality."

Davis nodded, feeling a connection that went beyond mere professional courtesy. "I'll see you in thirty minutes," he said, before turning and heading back to his own quarters.

Ingrid entered her room, taking a moment to gather her thoughts. She set her briefcase on the desk and began organizing the documents she would present. The files contained not only technical details about the U-boat but also historical context that would help the team understand the gravity of their discovery.

As she freshened up, Ingrid reflected on the importance of her mission. She had spent years uncovering secrets buried by time, but this U-boat represented something far more significant. It was a tangible link to a dark chapter in history, one that could have devastating consequences if not handled correctly.

Once she was ready, Ingrid opened her suitcase and took out a satellite phone. She pushed a few buttons and waited for a connection. After a moment, a male voice answered on the other side at which time Ingrid spoke. "It's me. Yes, I'm inside the research facility. From what I've heard from those assembled, they have found the missing U-boat."

The voice on the other end replied, too faint to be heard clearly through the thin walls of the room. Ingrid nodded, though no one was there to see it. "Understood," she said. "I'll keep you updated. This could be a significant find for us."

She ended the call and took a moment to compose herself, slipping back into her professional persona.

She gathered her documents and began preparing her presentation, the sense of dual purpose weighing heavily on her. To those at the research facility, she was a valuable ally. But in truth, her loyalties lay elsewhere.

Thirty minutes later, Davis knocked on Ingrid's door. She opened it, looking refreshed and ready. "Shall we?" he asked, offering a slight smile.

"Let's," she replied, returning his smile.

They walked together to the dining area, the buzz of conversation and clinking cutlery greeting them as they entered. The team was already gathered, a mix of anticipation and curiosity evident on their faces.

"As you can see Ingrid, everything is served here buffet style so please help yourself," Lena said. Everyone worked their way around the display of food filling their plates before returning to a long table.

Chapter 12

As they finished their lunch, a serious sense of anticipation filled the room. All eyes were on Ingrid, who had positioned herself at the head of the table. She turned her laptop screen towards the group of onlookers, which included Alina and other key staff members. The soft hum of the projector filled the room as the first slide appeared on the screen.

"Thank you all for your attention," Ingrid began, her voice clear and authoritative. "The information I am about to share comes from numerous sources, primarily Norwegian resistance members who were active in the area during the time the submarine was being created and later submerged. Their efforts to document and sabotage Nazi operations were instrumental in bringing this to light."

The first slide showed a grainy black-and-white photograph of a submarine partially constructed in a massive shipyard. "This," Ingrid said, pointing to the image, "is the U-boat in question, designated U-420, clearly visible on the conning tower. These photos were taken at great personal risk by members of the Norwegian resistance."

The next slide displayed several crew members standing on the deck of the U-boat. "Here, we see some of the crew. Notably, this man," she indicated a stern-looking officer in the center, "is Admiral Karl Weiss. He oversaw the production and outfitting of U-420, ensuring that it was equipped with the most advanced technology available at the time. I will come back to him later in my presentation."

The group leaned in closer, intrigued by the historical context. Ingrid advanced to the next slide, showing a younger man with a proud stance and piercing eyes. "This is Captain Hans Bauer, the commander of U-420. Bauer was known for his loyalty to the Nazi regime and his willingness to undertake missions that others deemed too dangerous. As you see, he had been awarded the Knight's Cross of the Iron Cross, the highest awards in the military and paramilitary forces of Nazi Germany during World War II."

Ingrid paused, letting the information sink in before continuing. "The most concerning aspect of this U-boat's mission was its involvement in experimental technologies. This brings us to Dr. Helmet Krieger, the scientist in charge of cryonics." She clicked to the next slide, revealing a photo of a bespectacled man in a lab coat, standing beside a group of uniformed officers.

"Dr. Krieger's work in cryonics was cutting-edge for its time," Ingrid explained. "His goal was to develop methods to preserve human life for extended periods, potentially allowing Nazi operatives to reemerge in the future. The implications of his experiments are both fascinating and deeply unsettling."

The room was silent, the weight of the revelation pressing down on everyone present. The next slide showed a diagram of the U-boat's interior, highlighting various sections that had been modified to house experimental equipment.

"These modifications," Ingrid continued, "were intended to support Dr. Krieger's experiments. The Norwegian resistance documented these changes, providing us with invaluable insights into the true purpose of U-420."

Alina raised her hand, her curiosity evident. "Ingrid, what do we know about the success of these experiments? Did Dr. Krieger's work actually achieve anything?"

Ingrid sighed, her expression somber. "The documents we've recovered suggest that some of the experiments were successful to a degree, but the true extent of their success remains unclear. What we do know is that U-420 was intended to serve as a mobile laboratory and a potential time capsule for Nazi ideology."

Commander Davis, who had been listening intently, leaned forward. "This information is critical. We need to approach the exploration of this U-boat with extreme caution, not only because of the potential booby traps but also because of the historical and possibly dangerous technologies it houses."

Ingrid nodded. "Exactly. The photos and documents I've shown you today are just the beginning. There are likely more secrets hidden within the U-boat, and it's our job to uncover them responsibly and safely." Ingrid stopped to take a sip of her coffee before continuing.

"Let's return to Admiral Weiss," Ingrid said, advancing to a slide showing a blown-up car with two Nazi flags on its front fenders. The image was stark and brutal, a testament to the violence of the times. She clicked to the next slide, which displayed the gruesome remains of the admiral.

"By chance, on the day the submarine was submerged and sealed, Admiral Weiss's car was ambushed. He had lowered the back window of his vehicle to allow smoke from his pipe to escape, giving a resistance fighter the opportunity to throw in a hand grenade."

"Wow. Nice reward for securing one of Hitler's weapons," Commander Davis said with a sneer on his face.

Ingrid nodded, her expression serious. "Before the SS could respond, the resistance fighter secured the admiral's badly damaged briefcase containing much of the information I have just shared."

She paused, letting the gravity of the situation sink in before continuing. "Now, regarding the crew of the U-boat, they were placed in hypersleep. This was one of the experimental technologies Dr. Krieger was working on. The intention was for the crew to be reawakened at a later date, potentially to carry out missions long after the war had ended."

"However, the exact mechanism for reawakening them was not detailed in the documents we have. This leaves us with a significant gap in our understanding and a potential hazard if any automated systems are still operational."

The room was silent, the weight of Ingrid's words hanging heavily in the air. The concept of a crew in hypersleep, waiting to be revived, was both fascinating and terrifying.

Ingrid advanced to another slide, this one showing schematics of the U-boat's interior. "Very little information survived about the booby traps, except for one dealing with the hatch in the conning tower. According to the documents, the hatch was rigged with an explosive device intended to detonate if opened improperly. This was likely a precaution to prevent unauthorized access and to protect the secrets within."

Commander Davis leaned forward, his expression intense. "We'll need to be extremely careful when approaching the hatch. If it's still active, it could pose a significant threat."

Ingrid nodded in agreement. "Exactly. Our priority must be to neutralize any traps before we proceed with a detailed exploration. We'll need to bring in EOD specialists to handle the hatch and any other potential threats we might encounter."

Alina raised her hand, her curiosity piqued. "Ingrid, do we have any leads on other possible booby traps inside the U-boat?"

Ingrid sighed, her expression thoughtful. "The documents we have don't provide specifics beyond the hatch. However, given the extent of the modifications and the paranoia of the time, it's reasonable to assume there could be more traps hidden within. We'll need to proceed with caution and assume the worst-case scenario."

Ingrid closed her laptop. The room remained silent for a moment, the gravity of their mission settling over them. With renewed determination, the team prepared to face the challenges ahead, united by a shared commitment to uncovering the truth and preserving history.

Commander Davis stood, his expression resolute. "Sometime this afternoon, explosive experts will arrive and together with my team, we will decide the best way to approach the U-boat. Let's get to work. We have a lot to do, and we need to ensure we're thorough and careful. Ingrid, your insights are invaluable. Thank you."

Ingrid offered a small, appreciative smile. "I'm here to help. Together, we'll navigate these dangers and uncover the secrets of U-420."

CHAPTER 13

As the dawn breaks over the fjord, a sleek black helicopter descends gracefully onto the makeshift helipad. Two distinguished figures step out, representatives from the Norwegian government, dispatched to oversee the operation and offer their expertise. The first is Major Henrik Thorsen, a stoic and seasoned officer with a wealth of knowledge on maritime operations. The second is Dr. Freya Nilsen, a renowned historian specializing in World War II artifacts.

Ingrid greets them with a formal nod, her eyes betraying a glimmer of relief. She quickly updates them on the situation, emphasizing the urgency and the collaborative effort required to uncover the U-boat's secrets.

In the briefing room, the research team, alongside the newly arrived Norwegian representatives, gather around a large table strewn with maps, photographs, and schematics. The atmosphere is charged with a mix of excitement and tension.

Major Thorsen begins, "We appreciate the efforts already made. Our priority now is to ensure the safe excavation of the U-boat while preserving any historical artifacts."

Commander Davis nods, turning the floor over to the explosive experts from the Navy SEALs who have just arrived. Chief Petty Officer Jake Mercer, a burly man with an air of quiet confidence, steps forward.

"We've reviewed the photos taken by Dr. Sousa," he begins, pointing to the images of the cement slab covering the U-boat. "Moving this slab is no small task. Raising it would be too risky and could damage the sub. Our proposal is to attach a heavy chain around the slab, leveraging the natural contours and strength of the surrounding area, and use tug boats to slide it out of the way."

Dr. Freya Nilsen interjects, "This method should minimize any impact on the U-boat and allow us to proceed with caution. We must also consider the potential booby traps mentioned earlier."

Chief Mercer continues, "Our EOD team will handle any explosives. Once the slab is moved, we'll deploy divers to carefully inspect the hull and ensure it's safe to proceed."

Commander Davis gets everyone's attention. "No one and I emphasis no one, is to attempt entry into the U-boat until I give the okay. Is that understood?" Everyone nods their head in agreement. Davis looks at his SEAL team explosive experts. "Okay, she is all yours."

The team moves to the dock, where tugboats are already stationed, their powerful engines rumbling in anticipation. The SEALs, clad in their diving gear, begin the meticulous process of attaching the heavy chains around the cement slab. Ingrid, Major Thorsen, and Dr. Nilsen observe closely, their expressions a mix of anxiety and determination.

Lena, Alex, Alina and Dr.Mueller watch from underwater video being supplied to the research center recording each and every move of the SEAL team.

With the chains securely in place, the tug boats begin to pull, the chains creaking under the immense pressure. Slowly but surely, the cement slab begins to shift, inch by agonizing inch. The tension is palpable as the team watches the progress.

Finally, with a loud groan, the slab slides free, revealing the weathered hull of the U-boat beneath. A collective sigh of relief sweeps through the group. As the divers conduct their initial inspection, Ingrid turns to Commander Davis. "We're one step closer, but the real challenge begins now. We must be prepared for anything."

Commander Davis nods, his gaze fixed on the newly exposed U-boat. He recalls the demolition experts and everyone gathers in the dining room area."Agreed. Let's regroup and plan our next move. This is just the beginning."

With each member present in the mess hall, everyone is acutely aware of the historical significance and the potential dangers that lie ahead. The path to uncovering the U-boat's secrets is fraught with peril, but they are determined to see it through, united in their quest for knowledge and discovery.

Everyone could hear the approach of a second helicopter. "That must be Chief Mercer and his team," Commander Davis announced. He left to group and went outside to meet the Chief and then escorted them into the command center where introductions were made.

In one corner, Commander Davis began talking to the EOD Inspection team about the current situation of the U-boat. Neither Lena or Alex could hear what was being discussed but they assume the topic was how to breach the U-boat. Finally, when their discussion ended, Davis turned and addressed the research team.

"With the cement slab now out of the way, Chief Mercer and his team of explosive ordnance disposal (EOD) specialists will begin their careful inspection of the U-boat at daybreak. Soon a submersible will arrive that has the ability to dock with the submarine. They will methodically, scan for any signs of booby traps or unstable explosives and make the initial entrance.

Chief Mercer looked at the group. "I assume you have a schematic drawing of the U-boat?" Both Ingrid and Dr. Mueller presented him with drawings of the U-boat. "Excellent. It looks like the Nazis made a few adjustments to their conning tower and that will be our point of entry."

A few hours later, a Boeing CH-47F Chinook helicopter arrived, its twin blades whipping up the sea water. Below was a heavy chain supporting a four-man submersible. The vehicle was released from the Chinook by Commander Davis' SEAL team and secured to the dock of one of the U-boat bunkers.

"We still have a lot of daylight left Chief. Do you want to go down and get started?" Davis asked.

"Absolutely," he replied, turning and selecting two other men from his team to accompany him down to the awaiting U-boat. They enter from the nearest U-boat bunker dock.

With communication established between the submersible and the research command center, Chief Mercer and his team directed the submersible down to the World War II relic.

"We've reached the boat. Our universal docking mechanism seems to be working....Okay, we are now attached to the U-boat," Mercer's voice said over the speaker.

Chief Mercer interjected, "The hatch in the conning tower appears to be rigged as we suspected. We'll need to disarm it before we can proceed since that is the easiest way to enter the sub."

Dr. Freya Nilsen steps forward, her eyes gleaming with the thrill of discovery. She addresses Commander Davis. "This U-boat is a treasure trove of history. Every detail we uncover will shed light on a pivotal moment in World War II. We must document everything meticulously."

"Understood, Doctor," Davis replied. "Dr. Lawrence and her team will be recording our progress both outside and inside the submarine. I suggest that we all start making our preparations for tomorrow and regroup here for dinner tonight."

CHAPTER 14

The Norwegian representatives, and the entire research staff are gathered around the communication command center listening for further updates from Chief Mercer.

The team holds their breath, knowing that the EOD experts are having to delicately manipulate the ancient, rusted mechanisms of the booby trap. Every click and creak echoes ominously in the silence, each movement laden with the potential for disaster. Seconds stretch into minutes, the tension mounting with every passing heartbeat.

Finally, Chief Mercer looks up, a bead of sweat tracing down his temple. He gives a slow, deliberate nod. "It's safe," he murmurs, his voice breaking the oppressive silence. "We dismantled the booby trap."

Cheers and back slapping break out in the research center. Everyone is imagining the next step by Chief Mercer and his team. The opening of the conning tower and entrance into the Nazi U-boat.

**

As they descend into the depths of the U-boat from the conning tower, the air grows thick with anticipation. The interior is eerily silent, a time capsule frozen in place. The walls are adorned with faded insignia and unsettling pictures of Adolf Hitler, while the air is tinged with the scent of rust and decay.

"Okay, the entrance to the sub is safe," Mercer said as he and his team head back to the submersible.

"Great job, guys. Please return to the research center for the next stage," Commander Davis called over the radio. "We need the scientists to be with you as the U-boat is examined to ensure no contamination occurs regarding historical integrity."

"Roger that. On our way," Chief Mercer responded.

Davis turned to Lena, Alex, and Dr. Mueller. "Well, now it is up to you three and Ingrid to decide how we should proceed, so be prepared to discuss it once they return. My men will enter first to locate and disarm any other booby traps. After that, as far as I'm concerned, investigate to your hearts' content."

"Thank you, Commander. We will get together with Ingrid as soon as possible and discuss how best to proceed. We will be prepared to make our presentation," Lena said.

**

The EOD team emerged from the U-boat and was immediately met by Commander Davis, his expression a mix of relief and curiosity. "Again, great job," he said, his voice steady. "What was it like below the conning tower?"

Chief Mercer, still shaking off the adrenaline, took a deep breath. "Commander, it was the scariest thing I have ever experienced. Descending into that U-boat was like climbing into a time capsule straight from 1944-45. The silence was haunting, almost as if the past was holding its breath. "

"Remarkably, with the small exception of rust on the top of the conning tower, the hull and interior are pristine. It's like stepping into another era, preserved perfectly in the cold grip of the deep, almost like it's been waiting for us, untouched by time."

Captain Davis nodded, absorbing the gravity of the discovery. "That sounds incredible. I know you and your team wanted to start searching the U-boat, but we need to ensure everything is documented accurately and handled with the utmost care. That order came directly from the top. This is a significant piece of history we're dealing with."

"I understand, but I assume we will be leading the team of scientists when they enter. The booby trap was quite elaborate and if detonated, the blast area would have been immense." Chief Mercer's eyes reflected the surreal nature of their find.

Commander Davis clapped Mercer on the shoulder. "Alright, get yourself and your crew inside and prepare for dinner. I'm having the scientists make a presentation afterwards, discussing the next phase. We're making history here, and we need to do it right."

**

Alex was lying on his bed, staring at the ceiling and replaying the day's events in his mind, when he heard a knock at the door. He opened it to find Lena standing there with a big smile on her face.

"Want some company?" she asked, her eyes twinkling with excitement. Without answering, Alex stepped aside and opened the door wider, inviting her in. Lena walked in and sat on the edge of the bed, her demeanor still buzzing with the day's discoveries.

"I can't believe how smoothly everything went today," Lena began, her voice tinged with awe. "It feels like we're on the brink of something monumental."

Alex nodded, sitting next to her. "It's surreal, isn't it? Seeing that U-boat, perfectly preserved, like it was waiting for us all this time. It's like we've unlocked a door to the past."

Lena sighed, leaning back slightly. "I know. It's hard to wrap my head around it. The history, the stories that submarine holds... it's overwhelming."

Alex looked at her, sensing a deeper thought. "You seem more excited than usual. What's going on in that head of yours?"

Lena chuckled, a touch of nervous energy in her laugh. "I feel like a kid again. You know, when I was little, the night before visiting Disneyland, I couldn't sleep at all. The anticipation, the excitement... that's how I feel right now. Knowing that tomorrow we'll be diving deeper into that U-boat, uncovering its secrets, it's just... I can't help but feel thrilled and anxious all at once."

Alex smiled, understanding completely. "Yeah, I get that. It's a mix of excitement and fear. The fear of what we might find, and the excitement of making new discoveries. It's what makes this work so addictive."

"Addictive. Yeah, that's the right word to describe how I feel," Lena said, her excitement palpable.

Alex smiled, a mischievous glint in his eyes. "I know of something else that's addictive and might help both of us sleep."

"Oh, do you now?" Lena replied, a playful tone in her voice as she moved closer. "Well, I think you should show me."

She jumped onto Alex's lap, their shared laughter breaking the tension of the day. For a moment, the weight of their mission faded, replaced by a lightness that was both comforting and invigorating.

Lena's smile softened, her eyes reflecting the shared sentiment. "I guess that's what drives us, isn't it? The unknown, the thrill of discovery. But it's also the responsibility. We have to handle everything with such care."

Alex reached out, giving her hand a reassuring squeeze. "We will. Together, we'll make sure everything is done right. We're a good team."

Lena squeezed his hand back, feeling a wave of gratitude and confidence. "Thanks, Alex. I feel better knowing we're in this together."

She stood up, a thoughtful look on her face. "I should probably try to get some sleep, even though I doubt I'll manage much. Tomorrow's going to be a big day."

Alex nodded, standing up with her. "Yeah, rest up. We'll need all the energy we can get."

As Lena walked to the door, she turned back with a smile. "Goodnight, Alex. See you bright and early."

"Goodnight, Lena," he replied, watching her leave with a sense of shared purpose and anticipation for what the next day would bring.

CHAPTER 15

As everyone gathered in the large dining hall, Lena started off the presentation for the scientists, having received their input. "Commander Davis, Chief Mercer, we are ready to explore U-boat 420, but an issue has arisen. The examination of the submarine will take weeks, if not more, and will require assistance from experts from both Norway and the United States. For example, none of us have the knowledge necessary to properly inspect the U-boat's nuclear reactor and its drive mechanism. Even the cryogenics is something beyond our expertise." She paused, allowing them to process what she had said.

"That said, going back and forth to the submerged U-boat by submersible will be tedious at best. Moreover, if dismantling various parts of the submarine becomes necessary, it would be impractical."

"So, what do you suggest?" Commander Davis asked.

Lena turned to both Drs. Nilsen and Mueller. Dr. Nilsen began to speak as Dr. Mueller unrolled an enlarged picture of the submarine. "What we propose is to surface the U-boat." Davis and Mercer stared at each other before returning their focus to Dr. Nilsen. "As Chief Mercer has stated, the submarine is structurally in excellent shape." She turned to Dr. Mueller.

"Gentlemen, what we are suggesting is that if we can obtain dredging equipment and use divers to remove the sediment under these three areas—the area containing the reactor, the area to the right of the conning tower, and here, under the torpedo room—we can create a plan to raise the U-boat."

Ingrid picked up the conversation. "Once the sediment is removed, we will insert ballast tanks—balloons, if you will—in those strategic areas. Inflating them slowly but simultaneously should free the U-boat, allowing her to rise to the surface."

Davis again turned to Mercer. "What do you think?"

"Ingenious plan, but there is one caveat. We've already found one booby trap. What if trying to raise the U-boat triggers other booby traps that we haven't found yet?"

Commander Davis paused, considering the gravity of the situation. "You raise a valid point, Chief. The risk is significant. However, I believe this decision goes beyond our immediate team. It's a matter for the Norwegian government and our own State Department. We'll need to consult with them before proceeding. We must ensure that all potential hazards are meticulously assessed and that we have the necessary approvals and support. This operation could have far-reaching implications, both in terms of safety and international relations."

Mercer nodded in agreement. "We should also consider involving additional experts in booby trap detection and disarmament. Their expertise could be invaluable in preventing any potential disasters during the raising process."

Davis turned back to the group, his expression resolute. "I'll initiate the necessary communications with our State Department and leave communication with the Norwegian government to you, Major Thorsen. In the meantime, we should prepare detailed reports outlining our findings and the proposed plan. Let's ensure we have all the information ready for a thorough review and risk assessment."

"I'm going to go ahead and request dredging equipment Who knows how long the various governments are going to take to give us permission, but let's assume they will," Mercer said.

The room was filled with a sense of determination. They knew the challenges ahead, but with careful planning and collaboration, they could overcome them and unlock the secrets of U-boat 420.

**

Twenty-four hours later, Commander Davis received an email from the State department. *"An agreement has been reached with the governments of the United States and Norway. All necessary methods should be utilized to raise the U-boat. A decision to notify the German government will follow the raising of their U-boat."* This time, for some unknown reason, the email was not signed but the email address was the same as before.

Commander Davis personally contacted the principal players involved in the operation to raise U-boat 420, outlining the plan for Chief Mercer and other SEAL divers to commence dredging operations. They scheduled a detailed briefing to take place at breakfast the following morning.

Over coffee at breakfast, Davis expressed his appreciation to Mercer. "Nice thinking about ordering the dredging equipment when you did. It saves us a lot of time," he said, taking a sip. "How much time do you think it will take to remove the sediment from those three areas?"

Mercer looked thoughtful. "I really won't know until we see what type of sediment is down there. It could be sand, which would make it quicker, but if it's clay, who knows. My main concern is keeping the balance of the U-boat once we start inflating the ballast tanks. If they have a booby trap that's attached to a gyro device, any dip of the bow or stern could set it off."

Davis nodded, understanding the complexity of the task. "We need to ensure that every step of this operation is meticulously planned. We'll monitor the balance of the U-boat continuously. Safety is our top priority."

Mercer agreed. "I'll have my team conduct preliminary dives to assess the sediment composition. We'll also run simulations to understand how the ballast tanks will affect the U-boat's stability. Once we have that data, we can refine our plan and address any potential issues."

Davis leaned back, contemplating the challenges ahead. "We should also consider setting up a contingency plan. If we encounter any unexpected difficulties, we need to have alternative solutions ready."

"Absolutely," Mercer replied. "We'll coordinate with the engineers and booby trap specialists to cover all bases. This is a delicate operation, but with careful planning and execution, we can manage the risks."

Davis finished his coffee, feeling a renewed sense of determination, before standing and hitting his coffee cup with a spoon, getting everyone's attention.

"Listen up, everyone. You probably see a few new faces among us. These are engineers who will work with Chief Mercer and the SEAL teams. I brought these experts in so that they can monitor the inflation of the ballast tanks as well as monitor the balancing of the U-boat as it rises."

"Why is that necessary?" Ingrid asked.

"If the Nazis have a booby trap that is geared to monitor the level of the U-boat in its current state, the rising of the bow or stern, if not done together, could activate the device." Ingrid nodded indicating that she had not thought of that," Chief Mercer responded.

"There is going to be a tremendous amount of activity in the closest U-boat bunker and where the divers will be conducting the dredging so I'm ordering everyone to remain inside the research center until the submarine surfaces."

He turns to Chief Mercer. "Okay, Chief. It is now if your hands," Commander Davis stated.

CHAPTER 16

As the day progressed, remarkable headway was made with the dredging of the sediment under the U-boat. After the SEALs successfully inserted the three large ballast tanks, everyone once again gathered in the main dining hall where Chief Mercer addressed the group.

"The ballast tanks are in place. So far, so good," Mercer began, his voice steady but serious. "After lunch, the tricky part begins. Several of my divers will remain on the bottom outside the sub, closely monitoring the inflation of the tanks. Engineers above will, upon my signal, start sending air to the tanks. They are confident that they can successfully inflate the tanks at the same pace, thus ensuring the U-boat remains balanced as it ascends to the surface. For those of you who pray, that will be the time."

He paused, allowing the seriousness of the situation to sink in. The room was filled with tense anticipation, everyone fully aware of the risks involved in the operation.

"We've taken every precaution we can," Mercer continued. "My team has run multiple simulations, and we've coordinated with the engineers to make sure we're all on the same page. But we're dealing with an old submarine and potential unknown booby traps. We need to be ready for anything."

Commander Davis stepped forward, reinforcing Mercer's words. "We have emergency protocols in place, and we'll be in constant communication with the divers and engineers. Our primary goal is to safely bring the U-boat to the surface and ensure everyone's safety throughout the process."

The room was filled with a mix of determination and apprehension. Each member of the team knew their role and the importance of their contribution to the success of the mission.

After lunch, the divers suited up and took their positions on the surface above the U-boat. The engineers made final adjustments to the air supply systems, ensuring everything was ready. Mercer gave a final briefing, reiterating the plan and emphasizing the importance of synchronized inflation.

As the divers descended and the engineers prepared to send air to the tanks, a solemn silence fell over the team. This was the moment they had been preparing for, and the stakes couldn't be higher.

"Remember," Mercer said, his voice calm but firm, "we're all in this together. Stay focused, stay calm, and we'll get through this."

With a nod from Davis, Mercer signaled the start of the operation. The engineers began to inflate the ballast tanks, and the team watched with bated breath as the U-boat slowly began its ascent.

The team held their breath as the engineers initiated the inflation of the ballast tanks. The sound of compressed air being released filled the air, echoing through the underwater environment. The divers stationed around the U-boat watched intently, their lights illuminating the dark waters and revealing the slow expansion of the massive tanks.

"Inflation has begun," reported one of the engineers through the intercom. "All systems are stable."

Chief Mercer, monitoring the situation from above, glanced at the various screens displaying the live feed from the divers' cameras. Every eye was on the tanks, watching for any sign of imbalance or potential danger.

"Keep it steady," Mercer instructed. "Maintain the pressure evenly across all tanks."

Minutes felt like hours as the tanks continued to inflate, the air pressure gradually lifting the U-boat from its resting place. Sediment and debris began to shift, creating a cloud of particles that momentarily obscured the divers' view.

"Visibility is low," one diver reported. "But the tanks are holding. No signs of instability yet."

The tension in the control room was palpable. Commander Davis paced back and forth, unable to take his eyes off the monitors. Each member of the team knew that one wrong move could spell disaster, not just for the U-boat but for the divers risking their lives below.

"How are we looking?" Davis asked, his voice tight with anticipation.

"So far, so good," Mercer replied. "The tanks are inflating at an even rate. We're still balanced."

As the tanks neared their full inflation, the U-boat began to creak and groan, the sounds of metal under stress echoing through the water. The divers reported the increasing noise, adding to the suspense of the moment.

"We're almost there," Mercer said, his voice a mix of hope and caution. "Everyone, stay sharp. We're not out of the woods yet."

Suddenly, a loud pop reverberated through the water, causing the divers to flinch. One of the ballast tanks had reached its maximum capacity, releasing a burst of air. The team above held their breath, waiting to see if the U-boat would remain stable.

"Status check!" Mercer barked.

"All tanks are holding," came the response. "The U-boat is starting to move."

The sediment around the U-boat's hull began to shift more noticeably, a clear sign that the submarine was breaking free from its decades-long resting place. The divers reported the movement, their voices tense but controlled.

"It's happening," one diver said. "The U-boat is lifting."

The control room erupted in a flurry of activity as everyone focused on the delicate process of guiding the U-boat to the surface. Mercer kept a close eye on the readouts, ensuring that the ascent remained smooth and controlled.

"Slow and steady," Mercer reminded the team. "We need to keep the balance as it rises."

The U-boat's rise was agonizingly slow, each inch gained a small victory against the forces of nature and time. The divers continued to monitor the tanks and the submarine's hull, ready to respond to any signs of trouble.

"Sediment is clearing," a diver reported. "We have better visibility now. The U-boat is moving smoothly."

As the U-boat continued its ascent, the control room watched in silent anticipation. The submarine, once a ghostly relic hidden beneath the ocean's depths, was now making its way back to the surface, guided by the meticulous efforts of the team.

"Prepare for final ascent," Mercer instructed. "Everyone stay focused. We're almost there."

The U-boat broke free from the last of the sediment, rising more quickly now as the ballast tanks reached their full capacity. The divers reported the increased speed, adjusting their positions to maintain a clear view of the submarine.

"It's clear," one diver said, the relief evident in their voice. "The U-boat is rising."

With a final creak and groan, U-boat 420 emerged from the depths, breaking the surface of the water. The team above watched in awe as the once-hidden submarine revealed itself, a testament to their determination and skill.

"We did it," Mercer said, a smile breaking across his face. "U-boat 420 is on the surface."

The room erupted in cheers, the tension giving way to celebration. The team had achieved what once seemed impossible, bringing the U-boat back to the light of day. But even as they celebrated, they knew their work was far from over. The mysteries of U-boat 420 awaited them, and the real exploration was just beginning.

CHAPTER 17

A party-like atmosphere continued in the research center and outside where Lena, Alex, Ingrid, Dr. Mueller and Dr. Nilsen had gathered to look at the now risen U-boat rising and dipping with the incoming waves.

The team stood on the dock of the closest U-boat bunker, gazing at the remarkable sight before them. U-boat 420, once entombed beneath layers of sediment and seawater, now floated majestically on the surface. The submarine's sleek, ominous silhouette was a stark reminder of its wartime past.

Lena couldn't help but feel a mix of awe and trepidation as she took in the details from her position on shore. Barnacles and seaweed clung to the hull, a testament to its long slumber beneath the waves. The conning tower, though weathered and worn, still bore the marks of its original craftsmanship.

"Unbelievable," Alex murmured beside her. "To think this has been hidden down there for so many decades and be in almost new condition."

Chief Mercer, still in his diving gear joins the group. "Give my team a little breather and we can enter the U-boat," he reported.

"You know, Chief, I have an idea. Let's get everyone back inside except what you consider should be a team standing watch," Commander Davis ordered.

The dining room away was a buzz with small talk everywhere. Commander Davis once again, got everyone's attention. "First, I want to congratulate Chief Mercer and his SEAL teams, plus the engineers manning the dredging and inflation of the ballast tanks." The room erupted into a few whistles an ovation. As the noise quieted down, Davis continued.

"I have made arrangements for the tugboats who helped remove the slab over the U-boat to return at 1 PM. At that time, they will direct the U-boat into the closest bunker where we can tie if off. By installing more lighting, your research can, if desired, go on 24/7." More cheers broke out. Davis turned to Mercer who gave him the thumbs up. "That said, let's get some food and drink and prepare to dock U-boat 420.

The scene was a coordinated symphony of precision and strength as two tugboats flanked U-boat 420, their powerful engines humming with exertion. The tugboats, positioned on either side of the submarine, worked in unison to guide the historic vessel back into one of the reinforced bunkers. The water around them churned and frothed, testament to the controlled power being exerted to move the submarine safely.

On top of the U-boat, SEAL team members stood ready, their eyes scanning both the vessel and the surrounding waters. They were a picture of calm focus amidst the bustling activity, their experience and training evident in their measured movements. Each member knew their role, ready to ensure the U-boat's transition from open water to the dock was seamless.

"Keep her steady," Chief Mercer called out, his voice carrying over the noise of the tugboats and the water. He stood at the conning tower, overseeing the operation with a practiced eye. The U-boat responded sluggishly, its massive bulk cutting through the water with a determined slowness.

As they approached the dock, the SEALs prepared the mooring ropes, coiling them with practiced ease. The dock was lined with support personnel, ready to catch and secure the lines that would tether the U-boat in place. The atmosphere was charged with anticipation; every movement was crucial in these final moments of the operation.

"Ready on the port side," one of the SEALs called out, securing his footing as the U-boat drew closer. He hefted the heavy mooring rope, his muscles tensed in preparation.

"Starboard side ready," another SEAL echoed, mirroring his teammate's actions.

With a final command from Chief Mercer, the tugboats adjusted their thrust, nudging the U-boat gently into position. The submarine glided towards the dock, its massive hull casting long shadows in the afternoon light. The SEALs swung into action, expertly throwing the mooring ropes to the waiting hands on the dock.

"Catch!" the SEALs shouted almost in unison, their ropes arcing through the air.

The dock workers caught the ropes deftly, quickly looping them through the mooring points and securing them with practiced efficiency. The thick, braided lines tightened, holding the U-boat fast against the gentle tug of the current.

"Port side secured," came the confirmation from the dock.

"Starboard secured," echoed the response, signaling the success of their efforts.

With the U-boat now firmly tethered, the tugboats eased their engines, the tension in the air slowly dissipating as the vessel settled into its new berth. The SEALs exchanged nods of satisfaction, their mission to guide the submarine safely completed.

Chief Mercer climbed down from the conning tower, a sense of accomplishment evident in his stride. He joined Commander Davis on the dock, where the two shared a brief handshake, acknowledging the success of the operation.

"Good work, everyone," Davis said, his voice filled with pride. "We've brought her home."

The team began their final checks, ensuring every line was secure and every precaution taken. As the evening light cast long shadows over the dock, U-boat 420 rested quietly in its berth, ready for the next phase of its exploration. The team, though tired, was filled with a renewed sense of purpose, knowing that their efforts had brought them one step closer to uncovering the secrets held within the submarine's ancient hull.

As the team gathered around the conning tower, Ingrid couldn't resist adding a touch of dark humor to lighten the tense atmosphere. "The only thing missing is a swastika flag flying from the conning tower," she remarked.

A few nervous chuckles rippled through the group, the tension breaking slightly.

Commander Davis stepped forward, his expression a mix of pride and determination. "We've done an incredible job so far, but now the real work begins. We need to document everything meticulously and ensure that the U-boat is stable and secure."

Dr. Mueller nodded in agreement. "We should start with a thorough exterior inspection before moving inside. We don't want any surprises."

The team split into smaller groups, each assigned a specific task. Lena and Alex began taking detailed photographs of the hull, capturing every inch of the submarine's exterior. Chief Mercer and his divers prepared to re-enter the U-boat, this time with more comprehensive equipment to facilitate their exploration.

As Lena focused her camera lens on the conning tower, she couldn't shake the eerie feeling that they were being watched. The history of the U-boat seemed to come alive around her, whispering tales of its wartime missions and the men who had once served aboard it.

"Hey, Lena," Alex called, breaking her reverie. "Look at this."

She turned to see him pointing at a series of strange markings on the hull, partially obscured by marine growth. "What do you make of these?"

Lena examined the markings closely. "They look like some sort of symbols or codes. We'll need to clean this area up to get a better look."

Ingrid joined them, peering at the markings with keen interest. "Could be anything from mission tallies to identification codes. We'll have to cross-reference with historical records."

Meanwhile, inside the U-boat, Mercer and his team moved cautiously through the narrow corridors. The air was thick with the scent of rust and decay, a stark contrast to the pristine condition of the cryogenic units they had discovered earlier. Every step was measured, every movement deliberate as they scanned for any remaining traps or structural weaknesses.

“Commander, this is Mercer,” his voice crackled over the intercom. “We’re inside and proceeding with caution. No immediate threats detected, but we’re taking it slow.”

“Understood, Chief,” Davis replied. “Keep us updated. We’re moving forward with the exterior analysis.”

Back on the deck, Davis coordinated with the engineers to stabilize the U-boat’s position. They set up a series of supports and anchors to prevent any unintended movement while the team conducted their investigations.

“Let’s make sure we get everything documented,” Davis instructed. “We’re making history here, and every detail counts.”

As the sun began to set, casting a golden glow over the scene, the team continued their meticulous work. The initial excitement had given way to a steady, determined focus. They knew that the secrets of U-boat 420 were waiting to be uncovered, and they were prepared to uncover them, no matter what it took.

CHAPTER 18

"So, the Nazis named it U-boat 420," Dr. Nilsen said, peering at the identification number etched into the conning tower. "I wonder if there was any significance to that number?"

"We found nothing regarding the numbering of the submarine in Admiral Weiss's documents, but it is interesting since it was Hitler's birthday," Ingrid replied, her brow furrowed in thought. "It could have no rational basis. Or, considering the state of Hitler's mind at the time, maybe the number 420 held some significance to him. We may never know."

As the team secured the U-boat, Commander Davis climbed up to the conning tower and placed a security team at the entrance. From his vantage point, he called down to those gathered on the dock. "First thing tomorrow morning, you'll be able to enter the U-boat, but only after the EOD team has checked out the area. We've already found one booby trap, so we need to be extremely cautious."

The team nodded in agreement, understanding the importance of safety in the face of potential dangers. Davis continued, his voice carrying a note of anticipation. "Now, let's go in and have dinner. I've arranged for a celebratory cake to be on display for everyone's enjoyment."

The mention of the cake brought smiles to the weary faces of the team members, a small but welcome reward for their hard work. As they made their way back to the main building, the atmosphere was filled with a sense of accomplishment and camaraderie.

Inside the dining hall, the team was greeted with a festive scene. A large cake, intricately decorated to resemble U-boat 420, sat at the center of the room. The cake was adorned with nautical designs, a fitting tribute to their efforts.

"Wow, that's impressive," Alex remarked, admiring the detailed decoration. "Who knew we'd be celebrating with a U-boat cake?"

Lena smiled, appreciating the lighthearted moment. "It's a nice touch. We deserve a little celebration after everything we've been through today."

As they gathered around the cake, Commander Davis raised a glass in a toast. "To the successful surfacing of U-boat 420, and to the hard work and dedication of each and every one of you. This is just the beginning of our journey. Cheers!"

"Cheers!" the team echoed, clinking their glasses together. The mood in the room was buoyant, the challenges of the day momentarily set aside as they enjoyed their well-earned celebration.

Over dinner, conversations buzzed with excitement about the next steps in their exploration. The team discussed their plans for the following day, eager to delve deeper into the mysteries of the U-boat.

As the evening drew to a close, Davis addressed the team one last time. "Get some rest tonight. We have a big day ahead of us tomorrow. Remember, safety first. We're making history here, and we need to do it right."

The team dispersed, their spirits high and their determination unwavering. As they headed to their quarters, the image of U-boat 420 breaking the surface remained fresh in their minds, a symbol of their incredible achievement and the promise of discoveries yet to come.

**

After the celebration wound down and the team began to disperse, Ingrid quietly slipped away, heading back to her quarters. The festive atmosphere had done little to ease the tension she felt, knowing the task that lay ahead of her. She needed to make a report.

**

Once inside her room, Ingrid locked the door and retrieved her satellite phone from a hidden compartment in her suitcase. The device was sleek and discreet, a tool of her trade. She glanced around the room one last time, ensuring her privacy, before dialing a familiar number.

The phone rang only once before a voice with a heavy Russian accent answered, "Report."

Ingrid took a deep breath, her voice steady as she began. "U-boat 420 has been successfully raised. The operation went smoothly, and it is now secured at the dock. We encountered no significant issues during the ascent."

There was a brief pause on the other end, then the voice prompted, "Details."

"The Americans inserted three large ballast tanks under the submarine and used controlled inflation to lift it. We monitored the process closely, and the U-boat is in remarkably good condition considering its time underwater. We secured it in one of the bunkers without incident," Ingrid continued, her tone professional and precise.

"And tomorrow?" the voice asked, a hint of impatience creeping in.

"Tomorrow, we will begin examining the interior of the U-boat. The EOD team will conduct a thorough sweep for any remaining booby traps before we proceed. I will be documenting everything meticulously and will report back with any significant findings," Ingrid replied.

“Understood. Maintain your cover and keep us informed,” the voice instructed before abruptly ending the call.

Ingrid stared at the phone for a moment, the weight of her secret mission pressing heavily on her. She had played her part well during the celebration, blending in seamlessly with the team, but she knew that her true purpose lay in what she would uncover inside U-boat 420.

With a sigh, she tucked the phone away and began to prepare for bed. Tomorrow would be another long and challenging day, and she needed to be ready for whatever they might find. As she lay down, her mind raced with possibilities, each one more intriguing—and dangerous—than the last.

**

There was a knock at the door, pulling Lena from her thoughts. She opened it to find Alex standing there, his eyes bright with excitement. “Hey, I wanted to see if you wanted to talk about tomorrow,” he said, stepping inside carrying two cups and a bottle of champagne.

Lena smiled, closing the door behind him. “I’m glad you came. I can’t stop thinking about what we might find in there. This is the kind of discovery that could redefine our understanding of that period.”

Alex nodded, his enthusiasm palpable. "Exactly. The technology, the history, it's all so incredible. And to think we get to be the ones to uncover it all."

They talked for a while sipping champagne, their excitement building as they speculated about the secrets the U-boat might hold. The anticipation of the next day's exploration was electric, each possibility more thrilling than the last.

As the conversation flowed, their shared excitement gradually turned into something more intimate. The intensity of the day's events, combined with their mutual passion for discovery, created a charged atmosphere. Without realizing it, they found themselves moving closer, their voices lowering, their touches lingering.

Lena looked into Alex's eyes, feeling a connection that went beyond their professional bond. She leaned in, and he met her halfway, their lips brushing tentatively at first, then more urgently. The worries of the day melted away as they gave in to the moment, their anticipation and excitement culminating in a passionate embrace.

They made love, their movements fueled by the adrenaline of their shared experiences and the promise of what was to come. In each other's arms, they found a moment of solace and connection, a brief respite from the weight of their mission and the secrets they both carried.

As they lay together afterward, the anticipation of the morning's exploration still lingered, but now it was accompanied by a sense of closeness and shared purpose. They drifted off to sleep, knowing that whatever the next day brought, they would face it together.

CHAPTER 19

The next morning, everyone was excited in advance of the entrance into the U-boat. Led by the EOD SEAL team, Chief Mercer and Commander Davis. Alex, Lena, Ingrid, and Dr. Mueller approached the open hatch of the U-boat. Ingrid, rudely, forced her way to the front of the line behind Commander Davis. The cold air outside and within sent a shiver down their spines as they prepared to delve deeper into the mysteries hidden inside the ancient submarine.

Chief Mercer, the head of the EOD team, descended first, his flashlight cutting through the darkness. The others followed cautiously, the echo of their footsteps adding to the eerie atmosphere.

"I sure hope no one suffers from claustrophobia." *He did* not expect a response. "Stay close and watch your step," Commander Davis instructed. "We don't know what other surprises might be waiting for us."

The SEAL team moved efficiently, their expertise evident in every movement. Within moments, they found a second booby trap—an intricate mechanism wired to the submarine's inner hull.

"Got something here," one of the SEALs called out, his voice steady despite the tension.

Chief Mercer moved in, his hands deftly working to disarm the trap. The team held their breath as he cut the final wire, the threat neutralized.

"That's number two," Mercer said, a hint of relief in his voice.

They continued deeper into the submarine, the air growing colder and more oppressive. The third booby trap was hidden near the reactor room, a complex web of wires designed to trigger an explosion.

"Another one here," Mercer announced, his focus unwavering.

Again, the team watched as he carefully disarmed the device, the tension in the air palpable. Finally, he stood up, signaling the all-clear.

"All clear. We can proceed," Mercer confirmed. The relief among the group was tangible as they resumed their exploration. The SEALs led the way, their flashlights revealing the submarine's secrets bit by bit.

They entered a large chamber dominated by an advanced-looking reactor. Dr. Mueller's eyes widened in astonishment. "This... this is a state-of-the-art nuclear reactor. Far beyond what we had at the time." Commander Davis looked at it.

"Dr. Mueller. This reactor rivals the ones we have."

Ingrid nodded, taking photos and notes. "It's incredible. The technology here is years ahead of its time."

Next, they found a stealth drive system, its sleek design a testament to the ingenuity of its creators. "This must have made the U-boat nearly undetectable," Alex speculated, marveling at the engineering prowess on display.

"Yes, I agree, yet with the exception of putting her through her paces after construction, it never really had a chance to set sail," Ingrid said.

As they moved through the submarine, they came across massive torpedoes, each one a deadly weapon capable of causing immense destruction. The sight was both awe-inspiring and chilling, a stark reminder of the U-boat's intended purpose. The sleek, metallic bodies of the torpedoes gleamed under the dim lighting, their deadly potential preserved through the decades.

"Everything looks brand new," Lena remarked, her voice echoing softly in the confined space. She didn't expect a reply, lost in her own thoughts as she marveled at the pristine condition of the weaponry and equipment.

The group continued their exploration, passing through narrow corridors until they reached the crew quarters. Commander Davis paused at the entrance, his brow furrowing in confusion. "Okay, this is strange," he muttered, stepping further inside.

"In what way?" Lena asked, following closely behind.

"The Chief and I have been in many submarines, and when you enter the crew quarters, each bed usually has personal items—pictures, letters, mementos from home," Davis explained, his eyes scanning the empty bunks. "But here, look. These beds look like they have never been slept in."

Lena looked around, noticing the stark emptiness of the room. The bunks were impeccably made, the sheets crisp and untouched. There were no signs of personal belongings, no indications that the crew had ever lived there. It was as if the quarters had been prepared for occupants who never arrived.

"It's almost like a ghost ship," she said quietly, a shiver running down her spine. "Why would a fully manned U-boat have crew quarters that look like this?"

Davis shook his head, his expression thoughtful. "It doesn't add up. We know there was a crew, and yet there's no evidence of them here. It's like they vanished into thin air."

The silence of the quarters felt heavy, filled with unanswered questions. As they moved deeper into the submarine, the sense of mystery grew. Every corner they turned, every room they entered, seemed to hold more secrets than the last.

Lena's mind raced with possibilities. Had the crew been forced to leave in a hurry? Had they never settled in at all? The U-boat was a puzzle, each piece leading them further into the unknown.

"Let's keep moving," Davis said, breaking the silence. "We need to document everything. There's a lot we still don't understand."

They continued their methodical examination, noting every detail and anomaly. The submarine, with its pristine yet eerie condition, was a paradox they were determined to unravel. The deeper they went, the more they realized that U-boat 420 was no ordinary vessel. It was a relic of the past, yes, but also a vessel shrouded in mystery, waiting for its secrets to be discovered.

Finally, they reached a sealed compartment at the back of the submarine. The door was marked with German writing, warning of the dangers within. Chief Mercer carefully opened the door, and after his team checked for more booby traps, everyone stepped inside.

The room was filled with cryogenic units, each one containing a member of the U-boat's crew. Captain Bauer lay in the central unit, his face peaceful and unchanged by time.

Lena gasped, her hand covering her mouth. "They look... they look like they haven't aged a day."

Dr. Mueller examined the units, his expression a mix of wonder and disbelief. "Cryogenic sleep. They must have been preserved since the war. This is unbelievable."

Ingrid approached Captain Bauer's unit, her face reflecting the weight of their discovery. "This is extraordinary. We've found not just a piece of history, but living relics of the past."

Commander Davis nodded, his eyes scanning the room. "We need to proceed carefully. The potential here is immense, but so are the risks."

As they stood in the heart of the U-boat, surrounded by the preserved crew and advanced technology, the team felt the enormity of their discovery. The past had come to life before their eyes, and the implications of their find were only beginning to unfold.

The team now faced the challenge of understanding and safely handling the technology and the cryogenically preserved crew. They would need to work together, combining their expertise to unlock the secrets of the U-boat and its inhabitants, all while ensuring the safety and integrity of their mission.

"Commander Davis, would it be possible for us to return to the research center to properly document what we've discovered so far?" Alex asked. "While we do that, Chief Mercer and his team can conduct another thorough search of the U-boat. Once they confirm it's secure, we can focus on examining each area in detail, starting right here. Properly examining and recording everything we're seeing will take a considerable amount of time."

Chief Mercer nodded in agreement. "I concur with Alex's suggestion, Commander. It's crucial we ensure the entire U-boat is secure before any detailed examination takes place. My team will conduct another sweep to make sure there are no additional threats."

Commander Davis looked thoughtful for a moment before nodding. "Alright, that sounds like a solid plan. Let's head back to the research center and start compiling our findings. In addition, please submit to me any other experts you would like to invite in your examination of the U-boat so they can be properly vetted."

Alex, Lena, Ingrid, and Dr. Mueller carefully made their way out of the U-boat, following Commander Davis. As they emerged into the crisp air, the weight of their discovery settled in. The enormity of what they had found was both exhilarating and daunting.

Back at the research center, they immediately began the meticulous task of documenting every detail. Photographs, notes, and sketches were compiled, ensuring that every piece of information was recorded accurately.

Chief Mercer and his team, meanwhile, re-entered the U-boat, their senses heightened as they methodically checked each compartment finding one final booby trap. The safety of the team and the preservation of the U-boat's secrets were their top priorities.

"The boat is clear, Chief," one of the SEAL team members reported.

"Very well. You all deserve some rest. Let's get back to the research center and I will check with Commander Davis to check on his future needs."

CHAPTER 20

Commander Davis sat with Chief Mercer over a cup of coffee, the rich aroma mingling with the crisp morning air. The two men, seasoned by years of experience, found a moment of solace amidst the ongoing investigation.

"You and your team did a hell of a job, Chief," Davis said, taking a sip from his mug.

"Thanks, Commander," Mercer replied, nodding appreciatively. "But there's something that's been bothering me since your observation about the U-boat almost being a ghost ship."

Davis raised an eyebrow, prompting Mercer to continue.

"Not only were the beds never used, but even in the officer's quarters, there was nothing there," Mercer explained, his voice tinged with unease. "It's as if the officers and crew never sailed the boat but were frozen or whatever the hell they call that."

Davis set his mug down, leaning forward with a thoughtful expression. "You're right. It's unsettling.

The quarters should have been full of personal items, traces of their lives on board. But instead, it's like they were prepared for a journey that never happened."

Mercer nodded, his brow furrowed. "And then there's the cryogenic units. The crew was preserved in perfect condition, but why? Were they never meant to wake up, or was something else at play?"

The Commander leaned back, considering the implications. "It's possible that they were part of some kind of experimental mission. The technology we've seen on this U-boat is advanced, even by today's standards. Maybe they were meant to be put into stasis for a long-term mission that never launched."

Mercer frowned. "But why leave everything so untouched? It's almost as if they knew they'd never actually live on the submarine. The whole setup feels more like a museum exhibit than a real living space."

Davis sighed, running a hand through his hair. "We need more information. We've barely scratched the surface of what this U-boat might be hiding. The logs, the equipment, everything we've found raises more questions than answers."

The two men sat in silence for a moment, the weight of their discovery pressing heavily on their minds. The U-boat, with its pristine yet eerie condition, was a riddle wrapped in an enigma, and they were determined to unravel it.

"We'll have to dig deeper," Davis said finally. "Every piece of this puzzle matters. We need to understand the purpose of this U-boat and what happened to its crew."

Mercer nodded. "Agreed. We'll keep at it. There's got to be something in there that will give us the answers we need."

As they finished their coffee, the sun began to rise, casting a golden light over the camp. The day ahead promised more challenges and discoveries, and both men felt a renewed sense of purpose. They were on the brink of uncovering something extraordinary, and they were ready to face whatever came next.

**

Surprisingly, the first scientist to make her way to the dining area was Ingrid. Spotting Commander Davis and Chief Mercer, she briskly walked up to them, her expression determined.

"Commander, would it be permissible for me to enter the submarine instead of waiting for the others?" she asked, her voice firm. "I work better by myself."

Davis glanced at Mercer before replying, considering her request. "My orders are to cooperate with all of the research staff and to ensure your safety. The Chief and his team conducted one additional search of the boat and have deemed it safe. So, to answer your question, be my guest, but make sure you take a flashlight."

Ingrid nodded, relief and determination mingling in her eyes. "Thank you, Commander. I appreciate it."

As she turned to leave, Davis added, "And Ingrid, stay in contact. Check-in periodically so we know everything is alright."

"I will," she promised, giving him a quick smile before heading towards the dock.

Mercer watched her go, a thoughtful expression on his face. "Nice looking lady. She's eager, I'll give her that. But why the rush to be alone?"

Davis shrugged, his gaze following Ingrid through the window as she approached the U-boat. "Maybe she thinks she can concentrate better without the others around. Or perhaps she's just that dedicated. Either way, we need to keep an eye on her."

**

Ingrid reached the U-boat and paused at the entrance, taking a deep breath. She adjusted her flashlight and double-checked her equipment before stepping inside. The dim light from her flashlight cut through the darkness, illuminating the narrow corridors ahead.

As she moved deeper into the submarine, the silence was almost oppressive, broken only by the sound of her footsteps and the occasional creak of the ancient vessel. Ingrid's mind raced with possibilities, each step bringing her closer to the answers she sought.

Entering the crew quarters, she couldn't shake the eerie feeling of the untouched beds especially after it was pointed out by the commander. The pristine condition of the rooms was a stark contrast to the idea of a fully manned submarine. It was as if the crew had never lived there, reinforcing the ghost ship analogy that had been mentioned earlier.

Ingrid took out her notebook, jotting down observations and thoughts. She meticulously documented every detail, her scientific mind working in overdrive. She knew the importance of thoroughness in her work, especially with such a unique and mysterious find.

As she continued her exploration, Ingrid couldn't help but feel a mix of excitement and trepidation. The U-boat held secrets that had remained hidden for decades, and she was on the verge of uncovering them. The anticipation was almost palpable, driving her forward with a relentless focus.

Finally, she arrived at the cryonics room. The whole area felt strange, as if the frozen crew were following her with their eyes. The eerie silence was punctuated only by the faint, steady rhythm of her own breathing. The room was bathed in a dim, cold light, casting long shadows that seemed to move on their own.

Ingrid's breath hitched as she took in the sight of the preserved crew, their faces serene yet haunting behind the frosted glass of their chambers. She, for some unknown reason, seemed to be drawn to the captain of the U-boat, now deeply asleep. The air felt thick with the weight of history, the unspoken stories of these men who had been trapped in time.

She began taking pictures and measurements, her hands trembling slightly. Each flash of her camera illuminated the room in harsh light, momentarily dispelling the shadows before they crept back in. She wasn't entirely sure what would be the most important to her handler, but she knew she had to document everything.

As she moved around the room, she felt an overwhelming sense of unease. The eyes of the frozen crew seemed to continue to follow her every step, their lifeless gazes piercing through the frost. Ingrid shivered, both from the cold and the unsettling atmosphere.

While adjusting her flashlight, she noticed a small panel embedded in the wall, partially hidden behind one of the cryogenic units. Curiosity piqued, she reached out to brush away the dust. As her fingers grazed the panel, she inadvertently pressed a hidden switch.

Unbeknownst to her, deep within the bowels of the U-boat, ancient mechanisms stirred to life. Cryogenic units, dormant for decades, began their slow reanimation. Temperature gauges adjusted, and a faint hissing sound, almost imperceptible, started as the thawing process commenced. The frozen crew, preserved in perfect stasis, were beginning to awaken.

Ingrid continued her exploration, oblivious to the chain of events she had set in motion. The eerie silence followed her, a constant companion in the dimly lit submarine. The U-boat seemed to pulse with a life of its own, the air subtly growing warmer as the cryogenic units did their work.

She moved cautiously, her nerves on edge. Every creak, every groan of the submarine's metal frame made her jump. The sense of being watched grew stronger, an unsettling feeling that gnawed at her resolve. She could not shake the impression that she was not alone, that the U-boat was slowly coming to life around her.

As she continued to document the cryonics room, the thawing process accelerated silently. Frost began to melt, and the once-frozen figures started to show signs of life. Ingrid's camera captured the condensation forming on the glass, the ice giving way to flesh.

The atmosphere grew increasingly oppressive, the air thick with anticipation and dread. Ingrid's every move felt amplified, the sound of her footsteps echoing ominously. She was on the verge of discovering something monumental, but she was also awakening a dormant past that might have been better left undisturbed.

Feeling queasy, she gathered her equipment and returned to the conning tower ladder, making her way out of the U-boat. Little did she know, the secrets of U-boat 420 were about to be revealed in ways she could never have imagined, as the frozen crew began their slow, inevitable return to consciousness.

CHAPTER 21

As Ingrid stepped off the U-boat and made her way back to the research center, the submarine's interior began to stir with life. The faint hissing of the cryogenic units grew louder as the thawing process continued. Metal creaked and groaned as the ancient mechanisms, dormant for so long, slowly reactivated. The air inside the U-boat warmed, and the frost that clung to surfaces began to melt, creating small rivulets of water that trickled down the walls.

Deep within the U-boat, the crew members began to awaken. The first to revive was the captain, his eyes fluttering open as he took a deep, shuddering breath. He struggled to sit up, his muscles stiff from decades of stasis. Around him, the rest of his crew were also stirring, their movements sluggish but growing stronger with each passing moment.

The captain, Captain Bauer, took a moment to regain his bearings. He looked around at his men, who were slowly coming to life, their expressions mirroring his own confusion and wariness. He called out in a hoarse voice, "Männer, wie fühlen Sie sich?" (Men, how do you feel?)

One by one, the crew responded, their voices weak but growing steadier. "Gut, Herr Kapitän," (Good, Captain) came the replies, accompanied by nods and attempts to stand.

Captain Bauer knew they needed to be prepared for whatever situation they found themselves in. His first priority was to ensure his men were armed. He gestured for them to follow him, leading the way to the armory. The crew moved with purpose, their training and discipline evident even after such a long period of inactivity.

In the armory, Captain Bauer distributed weapons to his men, checking each one to ensure it was functional. The familiar weight of the firearms brought a sense of reassurance to the crew. "Bleibt wachsam," (Stay vigilant) he instructed, his voice gaining strength. "Wir wissen nicht, was da draußen auf uns wartet." (We don't know what's waiting for us out there.)

With his men armed and ready, Captain Bauer decided to inspect the submarine's exterior. He made his way to the conning tower, noticing the hatch was ajar. Cautiously, he climbed the ladder, his senses alert for any signs of danger. As he emerged from the hatch, he was struck by the sight before him.

The U-boat bunker was as he remembered, but beyond it, he saw a modern research center, its lights glowing softly in the early morning light. The juxtaposition of the old and new was jarring, and Captain Bauer realized that significant time had passed since they had last surfaced.

He quietly lowered the conning tower hatch, securing it to prevent any unwanted entry. He needed time to understand the situation and formulate a plan. Returning to his men, he gathered them in the control room, their faces reflecting a mix of determination and unease.

"Wir sind nicht mehr in unserer Zeit," (We are no longer in our time) he began, addressing his crew. "Wir müssen herausfinden, was passiert ist und wer diese Leute sind." (We need to find out what has happened and who these people are.) His voice was resolute, the weight of their circumstances settling on his shoulders.

As the U-boat's systems continued to come to life, Captain Bauer and his crew prepared for the unknown. "Schalten Sie den Reaktor ein," (Start the reactor) Captain Bauer ordered, his tone firm. The crew sprang into action, following the command with practiced efficiency. The reactor, silent and powerful, began its operation, a faint vibration the only indication of its awakening.

As the U-boat's systems continued to come to life, Captain Bauer and his crew prepared for the unknown. The secrets of U-boat 420 were about to collide with the present, setting the stage for a confrontation that would span decades and test their resolve to the fullest. They moved with purpose, checking gauges and systems, ensuring everything was in working order.

Captain Bauer's mind raced with possibilities. Who were these people in the research center? What had happened to the world outside the bunker? He knew they needed answers, and they needed them quickly.

"Jeder bereit machen," (Everyone, get ready) he instructed, his voice echoing in the confined space. "Wir werden herausfinden, was los ist." (We will find out what's going on.)

As the submarine's interior hummed with renewed energy, Captain Bauer felt a surge of determination. They had survived this long, and they would face whatever came next with the same resilience and strength that had brought them through countless battles before. The secrets of U-boat 420 were no longer buried in the past; they were coming to light, and with them, the reawakening of an era thought long gone.

**

Back in her room, Ingrid grabs her satellite phone and dialed her handler's number, pacing the room as she waited for him to answer. The phone rang only once before the familiar voice answered, "Report."

"I went into the U-boat alone and begun preliminary examinations," Ingrid said, her voice steady. "But there's more inside than we anticipated."

"I need detailed information," the handler demanded. "You need to reenter the sub and gather more data. We need specifics—anything you can find."

Ingrid hesitated, knowing the risks, but her handler's tone left no room for argument. "Understood. I'll go back now." Driven by her handler's demands, grabbed her equipment, and headed back to the dock. The research center was still quiet, the morning light casting long shadows as she approached the conning tower of U-boat 420. She did not see either Commander Davis of Chief Mercer.

After reaching the conning tower hatch, she found it securely closed, a stark contrast to how she had left it. Ingrid frowned, her curiosity piqued. She reached out and began to fiddle with the hatch, trying to open it as quietly as possible. Despite her best efforts, the metal creaked and groaned, the sounds echoing eerily in the stillness.

Inside the submarine, Captain Bauer's senses were on high alert. "Quiet. Listen," he demanded. The noise from the conning tower interrupted his thoughts, and he motioned for his men to remain still. Grabbing his weapon, he moved towards the ladder, his eyes narrowed in suspicion.

As Ingrid finally managed to get a good grip on the hatch, she was able to pull it open, not realizing Captain Bauer had also turned if from the inside. She froze as the hatch suddenly opened, and Captain Bauer emerged, his weapon aimed directly at her.

"Wer sind Sie?" (Who are you?) he demanded, his voice cold and authoritative. "Was machen Sie hier?" (What are you doing here?)

Startled, Ingrid raised her hands in surrender. "I... I'm Ingrid, a researcher from the center. I mean no harm. I do not speak German."

Captain Bauer's eyes narrowed and in English told her to get inside now. He gestured with his weapon, forcing her into the U-boat. Once she was inside, he quickly secured the hatch, ensuring no one could follow.

Ingrid was led to the control room, where the crew watched her with wary and lustful eyes. Captain Bauer stood before her, his expression stern. "Explain yourself. What is this place? How did you find us?"

Ingrid took a deep breath, trying to steady her nerves. "We're researchers. We found your U-boat and raised it. We didn't know you were... alive."

As Ingrid spoke, Captain Bauer's expression changed from suspicion to realization. He translated her response to the crew. "How long have we been down here? What year is it? he asked, a hint of incredulity in his voice.

"Decades," Ingrid replied. "The year is 2024. The world has changed a lot since then."

Captain Bauer glanced at his men, then back at Ingrid. "You're staying with us until we figure this out. If you're lying, it won't go well for you."

Ingrid was confined to a small room within the U-boat, her mind racing with thoughts of escape and communication. Meanwhile, Captain Bauer and his crew gathered to discuss their next steps, the weight of their new reality pressing heavily upon them.

"We need to understand this new world," Bauer said, his voice filled with determination. "And we need to decide what to do next. The Fuhrer is counting on us."

"Captain, this is engineering. The reactor is at full capacity and the boat is ready to sail."

As the submarine's interior hummed with renewed life, the crew of U-boat 420 prepared to face a future they had never imagined, their fate now intertwined with that of the present day.

CHAPTER 22

Captain Bauer moved with purpose through the dimly lit corridors of U-boat 420. He knew time was of the essence. Turning to his two most trusted crew members, he issued a quiet command, "Ihr zwei. Entfernt unsere Festmacherleinen so leise wie möglich." (You two. As quietly as you can, remove our mooring lines.)

The two men nodded, climbing the conning tower with practiced stealth. Opening the hatch, they carefully scanned the area, ensuring it was clear before descending to the deck. Moving with silent efficiency, they untied the mooring lines and tossed them into the water. Upon returning to the control room, they notified the captain.

"Steuermann, langsame Fahrt voraus," (Helmsman, all ahead slow) the captain ordered.

"Langsame Fahrt voraus," (All ahead slow) the helmsman repeated. Silently, U-boat 420 slipped away from the bunker where its journey had begun in 1945.

Captain Bauer climbed to the conning tower, his eyes fixed on the research center receding in the distance. Once he was satisfied that they had put enough distance between themselves and the dock, he climbed down the tower and secured the hatch. "Vorbereiten zum Tauchen," (Rig for dive) he commanded.

The XO answered immediately, "Jawohl, Herr Kapitän. Vorbereiten zum Tauchen." (Aye, sir. Rig for dive.)

"XO, Tiefe auf 150 Fuß bringen. Tauchen, tauchen, tauchen!" (XO, make our depth 150 feet. Dive, dive, dive!)

**

Meanwhile, back in the research center, Commander Davis returned to the dining area to get another cup of coffee. As he poured himself a fresh cup, Chief Mercer rushed in, his face a mask of urgency. "Commander, the U-boat has sunk."

Davis stared at him, the coffee forgotten. "Sunk? Shit. How the hell did that happen?"

The two men sprinted outside, their hearts pounding with dread. They reached the dock and immediately saw the loose mooring lines floating in the water. Davis cursed under his breath, realizing the implications. "Someone threw off the mooring lines. They're gone."

Mercer looked out at the open water, frustration etched on his face. "We need to alert the authorities and get a search team out there. They can't have gone far."

Davis nodded, already moving towards the communications room. "We'll mobilize everything we've got. This just turned into a sub-hunt."

**

Underwater, the crew of U-boat 420 moved with the precision of a well-oiled machine. The submarine descended smoothly, the pressure gauges adjusting as they reached their target depth. Captain Bauer stood in the control room, his eyes scanning the various instruments and displays.

"Alles in Ordnung?" (Everything alright?) he asked the XO.

"Jawohl, Herr Kapitän. Alle Systeme funktionieren einwandfrei." (Aye, sir. All systems are functioning perfectly.) the XO replied.

Bauer nodded, a sense of grim satisfaction settling over him. They were back in their element, and despite the unknowns of the modern world, his crew was ready. "Wir werden herausfinden, was vor sich geht," (We will find out what's going on) he said to his men. "Und wir werden überleben." (And we will survive.)

As U-boat 420 continued its silent journey through the depths, the captain and his crew prepared for whatever challenges lay ahead, their resolve as steely as the submarine they commanded.

"Attention, this is the Captain. Our Fuhrer, Adolf Hitler, specifically picked us for this mission," Captain Bauer announced, his voice resonating through the submarine's intercom system. "This mission is of utmost importance for securing the future of the Fourth Reich. Our actions will pave the way for the resurgence of our nation's glory and power. I have been ordered to read you a letter given to me from Admiral Weiss."

He paused for a moment, the weight of his words sinking in among the crew. The men stood at attention, their faces a mix of determination and reverence.

Unfolding the letter with care, Captain Bauer continued, "In this letter, Admiral Weiss expresses his unwavering confidence in our success. He reminds us of the sacrifices made by our comrades and the necessity of our mission. We are the chosen few, entrusted with the vital task of ensuring the rebirth of our Reich. The eyes of history are upon us, and we must not fail."

The crew listened intently, their resolve hardening with each word. The captain's speech ignited a sense of purpose within them, a reminder of their duty to their nation and their leader.

"As we proceed with our mission, remember that our success will bring about a new dawn for our people. We are the vanguard of the Fourth Reich, and our actions will secure its rise from the ashes of the past. Our loyalty, our courage, and our dedication will be the foundation upon which our future is built."

Captain Bauer's eyes met those of his crew, his voice firm and resolute. "Now, join me in pledging our allegiance to the Fuhrer."

In unison, the crew raised their right arms in the Nazi salute, their voices echoing through the submarine. "Heil Hitler!" they proclaimed, their pledge a powerful affirmation of their commitment.

As the echoes faded, a steely silence filled the control room. The men of U-boat 420 were ready to fulfill their mission, their allegiance to the Fuhrer unwavering and their resolve unbreakable. The future of the Fourth Reich depended on their success, and they would stop at nothing to achieve it.

CHAPTER 23

Commander Davis contacted the State Department and the Norwegian government to report the disappearance of U-boat 420. The urgency in his voice conveyed the gravity of the situation.

"This is Commander Davis from the research center. We have an emergency situation. U-boat 420 has disappeared. We need immediate assistance to track it down. Our radar equipment is not the best to track its path."

As Davis was finishing up his phone call with the state department, Lena and Alex continued to monitor the radar screen in the command center. "Commander, I think I've got something. A faint signal heading northeast," Alex shouted.

Davis and Chief Mercer joined them looking at the radar screen. "Looks like they are currently heading north. I will pass that on to my supervisor," Commander Davis said as he reached for his phone.

**

Captain Bauer stood in the control room, his face a mask of determination. He knew that in order to stay undetected, they needed to use their most advanced technology. Turning to his helmsman, he issued the critical command.

"Steuermann, aktivieren Sie den Tarnmechanismus." (Helmsman, engage the stealth mechanism.)

The helmsman nodded, his fingers flying over the controls. "Tarnmechanismus aktiviert, Herr Kapitän." (Stealth mechanism engaged, Captain.)

As the U-boat's systems hummed to life, the entire submarine began to shimmer, gradually fading into invisibility. Bauer watched the transformation with a grim sense of satisfaction.

"Gut. Jetzt können wir unbemerkt bleiben." (Good. Now we can remain undetected.) He turned to the crew, his voice steady and commanding. "Wir müssen vorbereitet sein. Bleiben Sie wachsam und bereit für das Unbekannte." (We must be prepared. Stay vigilant and ready for the unknown.)

**

Lena Lawrence was monitoring the radar screen when she noticed something unusual. The blip representing U-Boat 420 was fading, becoming increasingly faint until it disappeared entirely.

"Commander Davis! Chief Mercer! Come look at this!" Commander Davis and Chief Mercer rushed over to Lena's station, their eyes scanning the screen.

"What is it, Lena?" Commander Davis asks.

Lena pointed at the radar screen, her voice tense. "The U-boat... it's gone. One minute it was there, and now it's vanished."

"That's impossible. Submarines don't just disappear, Dr. Mueller stated.

"Unless they have some kind of stealth technology," Davis replied.

Lena nodded, her expression serious. "It must be. They've activated something to make themselves invisible."

"Damn it. This complicates things. We need to update the State Department and the Norwegian authorities immediately. If they have this kind of technology, it makes them even more dangerous," Davis said and he again grabbed his phone.

"Lena, keep monitoring the screens. Any flicker, any sign of movement, I want to know immediately," Davis ordered.

"Yes, sir."

As Commander Davis headed to the communications room to relay the new development, Alex and Chief Merceer stayed with Lena, their minds racing through possible scenarios. The disappearance of the U-boat had turned an already critical situation into a high-stakes game of cat and mouse.

**

Captain Bauer watched the sonar display, confirming that their stealth technology had successfully rendered them invisible to external tracking systems. He went into the room holding Ingrid, who was still bound and watched by his crew.

Captain Bauer watched the sonar display, confirming that their stealth technology had successfully rendered them invisible to external tracking systems. He turned to Ingrid, who was still bound and watched by his crew.

“You see, Fräulein, we are not as outmatched as you might think. Our technology gives us the upper hand. Now, you will tell me everything you know about this world we have awakened in.”

Ingrid remained silent, her eyes defiant. Bauer’s expression darkened as he sighed and turned to his XO.

“Begin the interrogation. We need all the information we can get.”

The XO nodded, stepping forward with a cold, calculated demeanor. Without warning, he slapped Ingrid across the face, the force of the blow causing her mouth to bleed. He leaned in close, his voice menacing. “Shall we start again?”

**

The atmosphere in the research center was tense, a palpable sense of urgency gripping everyone present. Researchers and technicians were at their stations, eyes glued to their screens, waiting for any sign of the elusive U-boat. Lena's focus was unwavering as her hands hovered over the controls, monitoring the radar for any anomalies.

"Commander, I've sent a distress signal to the nearby naval base. They're on high alert and will assist in the search," Lena reported, her voice steady despite the tension.

"Good. Several Lockheed P-3 Orions are on their way to the area. We need all the help we can get. Keep trying to reacquire the signal. They can't stay invisible forever," Commander Davis responded, his tone firm and resolute.

Lena hesitated for a moment before speaking up, a slight blush creeping over her cheeks. "Commander, I'm embarrassed to say that I don't know what a P-3 Orion is."

Commander Davis gave her a reassuring nod. "Sorry. It's an Air Force aircraft, also known as a sub chaser. It's equipped with instruments able to detect the magnetic anomaly of a submarine in the Earth's magnetic field. Since we are dealing with a World War II U-boat, it should be easy for them to be spotted."

Lena furrowed her brow, considering his words. "Okay, but isn't this the same World War II U-boat that has just enabled some sort of stealth technology making it virtually invisible?"

Commander Davis paused, acknowledging the gravity of her point. "Good point, Lena. This changes the game. We'll need to rely on every resource at our disposal to track them down. Stay vigilant and keep monitoring for any irregularities."

As the minutes ticked by, the research center buzzed with activity. The team worked tirelessly, their determination fueled by the urgency of the situation. Despite the advanced stealth technology of the U-boat, they were resolute in their mission to locate and neutralize the threat.

CHAPTER 24

The atmosphere inside U-boat 420 was tense as the crew went about their duties with grim determination. The stealth technology had rendered them invisible to external detection, but the sense of urgency remained palpable. Captain Bauer stood in the control room, his mind focused on the mission ahead.

The XO approached, his expression serious. "Herr Kapitän, she is ready to talk."

Captain Bauer's eyes narrowed. "Good. Take me to her."

The XO led Bauer through the narrow corridors of the submarine to a small, dimly lit room where Ingrid was being held. As Bauer entered, he immediately noticed the state she was in. Her blouse was torn open, exposing her bra, and several lacerations marred her face. One eye was nearly swollen shut, and her breathing was ragged.

Bauer stood before her, his gaze cold and calculating. “So, Fräulein, you have decided to cooperate.”

Ingrid lifted her head, defiance still flickering in her eyes despite her battered condition. “I will tell you what you want to know. The year is 2024.”

Bauer’s expression hardened. “2024... What has become of Nazi Germany? What happened to the war?”

Ingrid took a deep breath, wincing at the pain. “The war ended in 1945. The Allies won. Germany was divided, and the Nazi regime was dismantled. Adolf Hitler is dead.”

The captain’s face twisted with a mix of disbelief and anger. “Impossible. Dr. Goebbels told us that we were on the brink of victory. How could this happen? How did our Fuhrer die?”

Ingrid’s voice was steady as she continued. “The Allied forces were too strong. They overpowered the Axis powers and liberated the occupied territories. The Russian invaded Berlin but before they reached the Fuhrerbunker, Hitler who married Eva Braun, both committed suicide. After the war, with the Allies in control of Germany, it was split into East and West, and the Nazi leaders were tried for their war crimes.”

Bauer’s fists clenched at his sides. “And the Third Reich? What of our vision for the future?”

Ingrid met his gaze, unwavering. “There is no Third Reich. The world has moved on. Germany is now a democratic country, and the ideals of the Nazi regime are condemned worldwide."

Bauer's eyes blazed with fury, but he forced himself to remain composed. "We shall see about that. Our mission is not over. We will find a way to reclaim our place in history."

Ingrid watched him, a mixture of fear and resolve in her eyes. "You can't change the past. The world won't allow it."

Bauer turned to the XO. "Prepare the crew for the next phase of our mission. We must gather more information and find our allies in this new world."

The XO nodded. "Jawohl, Herr Kapitän. Do you plan to tell them about our Fuhrer?"

Bauer hesitated before he spoke. "I am not sure at this time, so keep this information between us. Understood?"

"Jawohl, Herr Kapitan," he replied as he left the Captain with Ingrid.

Bauer cast one last look at Ingrid. "Remember, Fräulein, your cooperation ensures your survival. Do not test my patience."

Ingrid remained silent, her gaze defiant even in the face of her ordeal. The future was uncertain, but she knew she had to find a way to survive and stop whatever plans Bauer had in store.

**

Captain Bauer stepped into his cabin, closing the door behind him with a heavy sigh. The room was sparse, reflecting the utilitarian nature of life aboard a U-boat, but there was one item that stood out among the gray steel walls—a framed photograph of Adolf Hitler. Bauer walked over to it, staring at the image with a mix of reverence and longing.

He traced a finger over the glass, lost in thought. Memories of the former glory of the Third Reich flooded his mind. He recalled the grand parades, the fervent speeches, and the unyielding belief in their cause. For Bauer, those were the days of pride and power, when the world trembled before them.

The reality of Ingrid's words weighed heavily on him. The Third Reich had fallen, Hitler was dead, and their vision had been dismantled. Yet, Bauer's resolve only hardened. He turned away from the photograph, his face set in grim determination.

Beneath his bed, hidden from prying eyes, was a safe. No researcher or SEAL team member had discovered it during their initial explorations. Bauer knelt down and carefully unlocked the safe, pulling out a single envelope marked "Geheim" (Top Secret) in bold German script. He opened the envelope, unfolding the orders that had been entrusted to him decades ago.

As he read the documents, his eyes gleamed with a renewed sense of purpose. His mission was clear: to sail towards Great Britain and, once in position, launch a V-4 rocket into the heart of London. This would be Hitler's revenge against the British, a final act of defiance from beyond the grave.

The new and improved V-4 rocket contained a massive amount of destructive power, far surpassing the capabilities of the previous V-2 rockets. Unlike its predecessors, the V-4 was equipped with an advanced propulsion system that allowed for greater range and accuracy.

Its warhead carried a devastating payload of explosives and incendiary materials, designed to cause maximum destruction upon impact. Furthermore, the V-4 incorporated cutting-edge guidance technology, making it almost impossible to intercept or divert once launched. This new weapon represented the pinnacle of Nazi engineering, a testament to their relentless pursuit of superiority.

Captain Bauer knew that with such a weapon at his disposal, he had the means to deliver a blow that would echo through history, cementing the legacy of the Third Reich in a blaze of fire and ruin.

But the orders didn't end there. After the destruction of London, Bauer was to set his sights on three more targets—Moscow, Washington D.C. and New York City. The scale of the operation was immense, and the potential for chaos and destruction was unparalleled. Bauer's heart pounded with a dark excitement.

He knew the risks, but he also knew the potential impact. The world had moved on, but Bauer was determined to remind them of the might of the Reich. He folded the orders back into the envelope and returned it to the safe, locking it securely.

As he stood, he glanced once more at the photograph of Hitler. "Für das Reich," he whispered, a solemn vow to see his mission through to the end.

Bauer returned to the control room, his mind clear and focused. The crew needed to be prepared for the journey ahead. He would share his orders with them in due time, but for now, they needed to maintain their stealth and gather as much information as possible.

"XO," he called, his voice steady and commanding.

"Jawohl, Herr Kapitän," the XO responded, snapping to attention.

"Prepare the crew for a long journey. We have a mission to complete, and we must be ready for anything."

"Jawohl, Herr Kapitän."

Bauer stood in the control room, surrounded by his loyal crew. The path ahead was fraught with danger, but he felt a renewed sense of purpose. The world might have forgotten the Third Reich, but he was determined to ensure that its memory lived on, etched in fire and fury.

As U-boat 420 continued its silent voyage through the depths, Bauer's mind was filled with plans and strategies. The future was uncertain, but one thing was clear: he would stop at nothing to fulfill his mission and reclaim the glory of the Reich.

CHAPTER 25

The atmosphere inside the research center was electric with tension and urgency. Commander Davis, standing at the head of the room, addressed the gathered team. Scientists, military personnel, and researchers were all present, their faces reflecting a mix of anxiety and determination.

"Everyone, attention please," Davis began, his voice steady despite the gravity of the situation. "I have just been informed that the P-3 Orions are now actively searching the last known location of U-Boat 420. These aircraft are equipped with advanced sonar and magnetic anomaly detection systems, which should help us locate the submarine."

A murmur of acknowledgment rippled through the room. Alex stood next to a large table covered with maps and charts. Lena, the marine biologist turned submarine tracker, was by his side, her face still showing signs of worry but also determination.

"Let's go over what we know," Alex said, spreading a map of the North Atlantic across the table. "We need to figure out where they might be heading and what their mission could be." Davis a Chief Werner joined them.

Davis leaning over the table. "We know they have advanced stealth technology, but they can't stay hidden forever. They need to surface periodically for air, and that gives us windows of opportunity to track them."

Lena pointed to several marked locations on the map. "Their last known position was here, near the research center. If they maintain a northeasterly course, they could be heading towards the British Isles."

Alex frowned, considering the possibilities. "Why would they head there? What strategic value does that area hold for them?"

Davis sighed, rubbing his temples. "Remember, we're dealing with a crew from the 1940s. Their objectives might be rooted in the mindset of World War II. They could be trying to strike at a significant target, something that would have been crucial back then."

Lena's eyes widened with realization. "London. If they were trying to strike at a major Allied power, London would be an obvious target."

Commander Davis nodded, a grim expression on his face. "And if they have a weapon aboard... something more powerful than what they had in the 1940s, it could be devastating."

Davis turned to the team, his voice firm. "We need to consider all possibilities. They could also be heading to find old allies or resources. We have to cover every angle. What about Washington D.C., New York City, Moscow? They were significant targets during the war as well."

A young researcher spoke up, her voice shaking slightly. "If they have modern guidance systems, they could hit any of those targets with precision. We need to alert the relevant authorities and coordinate with naval and air forces to cover these critical areas."

Davis nodded, appreciating the input. "We'll send out alerts to all potential target locations. Meanwhile, we need to use every resource at our disposal to track their movements. Satellite imagery, sonar buoys, anything that can help us predict their next move."

Alex tapped on a spot on the map. "What about their need to resupply? Even with advanced technology, they'll need food, water, and other essentials. They might head towards less monitored areas where they can lay low and resupply."

Lena added, "Or they might have caches from their era, stashed in remote locations. We need to think like they would—strategically and resourcefully."

Davis stood straight, looking around the room at his assembled team. "Alright, everyone. Let's split into task forces. Some of you will continue analyzing historical data and potential targets. Others will work with the Navy and Air Force to coordinate the search efforts. Stay vigilant, and keep communication lines open. Every second counts."

As the team dispersed to their assignments, the weight of the task ahead pressed on them. The race to locate U-Boat 420 was not just a matter of historical curiosity—it was a critical mission to prevent a potential disaster. The shadow of the past had reemerged, and they had to stop it before it could cast its dark pall over the present.

**

The confined space of U-boat 420 hummed with the low vibrations of the engines. The XO, Lieutenant Heinrich, approached Captain Bauer with a grim expression. "Captain, we have a problem," he said, voice lowered to avoid alarming the crew.

Bauer looked up from his maps, his piercing eyes locking onto Heinrich. "What is it?"

"The cook has checked our food supply and found it rancid. The fresh drinking water also needs to be replaced.

Bauer frowned, absorbing the gravity of the situation. Supplies were crucial for their mission's success, and their isolation meant limited options. "Understood. We have no choice. We must raid a coastal town."

A young sailor, huddled over a map nearby, looked up and pointed to a spot. "Captain, there's a small town here, just a few miles inland. It should have what we need."

Bauer looks at the map and nodded . "Set a course for the town. Maintain our stealth maneuvers. We cannot risk detection."

The orders were relayed, and the U-boat began its silent glide towards the coast. The tension on board was palpable as the crew prepared for the raid.

"XO" Bauer called, "assemble a raiding party. They are to load up on food, water, and any communications they find, such as newspapers and radios. Anyone they come in contact with must be eliminated to keep our mission top secret."

The XO nodded sharply and went to gather the men. The raiding party was briefed, armed with automatic weapons, and ready to disembark as night fell. The small inflatable boats were lowered into the water, and the men paddled silently to the shore.

**

They found the town dark and still, except for a single grocery store with lights on. Inside, a few late-night shoppers and staff were unaware of the danger approaching. The raiders moved quickly, rounding up the occupants and herding them to the back of the store.

Shots rang out, muffled by the store's walls. The bodies were left behind as the men collected as much as they could carry—canned goods, bottled water, and other supplies. They also seized two computers, though their purpose was unclear to the sailors.

Back on the U-boat, the tension was high as the crew awaited the raiding party's return. Ingrid, a civilian scientist onboard, approached Captain Bauer, clearly distressed.

"Captain. Our captive is yelling that she needs to use the bathroom," a young crewmember named Hans states.

Captain Bauer opens the door to the room of Ingrid's confinement.

"Captain, I need to use the bathroom and get some water," she complained.

Bauer, already on edge, motioned to Hans. "Take her to the bathroom and see that she gets what she needs."

Hans nodded and led Ingrid down the narrow corridor. Once they were alone, Ingrid seized the opportunity to engage the sailor. "Thank you," she said, her voice softening. "This whole situation has been so stressful. It's nice to have someone to talk to. Do you speak English?"

The sailor, slightly taken aback by her tone, glanced at her nervously while displaying a smile and looking at her bra. "I speak a little," he replied with a heavy German accent.

"My name is Ingrid. What is yours?"

"My name is Hans."

"Nice to meet you, Hans," Ingrid replied as she entered the bathroom and closed the door. Hans remained outside on guard. Ingrid looked in the mirror and was shocked at her face and eye being so swollen. She used the toilet, but before flushing it, washed her face. The cool water felt good. She again looked in the mirror and saw that most of her blood had been removed.

Determined to use whatever advantage she could, Ingrid attempted to look as attractive as possible by pulling down her bra as far as it would go to emphasize her cleavage. Another lookover and she flushed the toilet and opened the bathroom door.

"Thank you, Hans. Now all I need is some water and food." She could see that Hans's eyes were fixated on her chest before he escorted her back to her confinement room, where he handed her a glass of water.

"Food will come later," Hans said, still looked at Ingrid's cleavage.

"Again, thank you, Hans. You are a very nice individual."

Hans looked visibly flustered, his eyes darting away from her gaze. "Just following my orders," he mumbled.

Ingrid leaned in slightly, her eyes glinting in the dim light. "You've been very kind. It's not easy for any of us, is it?"

The sailor swallowed hard, his duty conflicting with the unexpected attention. “No, it’s not,” he admitted, his guard beginning to lower.

Ingrid smiled, sensing his discomfort. “Maybe you could help make things a bit more bearable for me?” she suggested, her voice dripping with subtle suggestion.

The sailor’s face flushed, but he nodded. “I’ll do what I can.”

As Ingrid was escorted back to her quarters, the raiding party returned, laden with supplies. Bauer breathed a sigh of relief as they unloaded the goods, but his mind was already racing ahead, planning their next move. They had secured their immediate needs, but the mission was far from over.

The crew worked quickly to stow the supplies and integrate the new intelligence materials. The seized computers, though unfamiliar, were handed over to the crew for examination.

Captain Bauer stood on the deck, staring into the night. The raid had been successful, but the stakes were higher than ever. He knew that the secrecy of their mission was paramount, and the slightest mistake could spell disaster.

As the U-boat slipped back into the depths, the crew settled into their routines, each man aware of the fine line they walked between success and catastrophe. And amidst it all, Ingrid’s interaction with the sailor added an unpredictable element to the already tense atmosphere, one that Bauer would have to manage carefully in the days ahead.

**

The crew worked quickly to stow the supplies and integrate the new intelligence materials. The seized computers, though unfamiliar, were handed over to the more tech-savvy members of the crew for examination.

Captain Bauer stood on the deck, staring into the night. The raid had been successful, but the stakes were higher than ever. He knew that the secrecy of their mission was paramount, and the slightest mistake could spell disaster.

As the U-boat slipped back into the depths, the crew settled into their routines, each man aware of the fine line they walked between success and catastrophe. And amidst it all, Ingrid's interaction with the sailor added an unpredictable element to the already tense atmosphere, one that Bauer would have to manage carefully in the days ahead.

CHAPTER 26

The atmosphere in the research center was heavy with a sense of stoic boredom and unease. The constant hum of machinery and the occasional clinking of tools were the only sounds breaking the oppressive silence. The team, having exhausted their immediate tasks, found themselves in a state of restless inactivity.

Lena sat at a cluttered desk, absentmindedly flipping through her notes. Across from her, Alex was tinkering with a piece of equipment, his brow furrowed in concentration.

"Alex, do you ever get the feeling we're missing something? Like there's a piece of the puzzle right in front of us, but we just can't see it?" Lena asked, breaking the silence.

Alex looked up, a thoughtful expression on his face. "All the time. Especially with the pressure we're under. It's hard to stay focused when we're just waiting for the next big thing to happen."

Lena nodded, glancing around the room. "I just wish we had something concrete to work on. This waiting is driving me crazy."

Before Alex could respond, Alina, Lena's assistant and back up communications officer, entered the room, her face pale and tense. "I just received word that a grocery store was raided on a small island in the Faroe Islands of Denmark," she announced.

The room fell silent as everyone turned to look at her. "What happened?" Lena asked, her voice barely above a whisper.

Alina took a deep breath. "The raiders rounded up the shoppers and staff in the back of the store and shot them. It's believed to be the work of the U-boat we've been tracking."

"How do they know it is the Germans?" Davis asked.

"Witnesses saw them hurriedly leave the store and row out to a submarine offshore. It has to be them." Alina responded.

Chief Mercer and Commander Davis exchanged worried glances before rushing to the map pinned on the wall. They quickly traced the U-boat's route, their fingers moving over the vast expanse of ocean.

"Unbelievable," Chief Mercer muttered. "The amount of distance this U-boat has covered is astounding."

Commander Davis nodded, his expression grim. "We need to recalibrate our projections. They're moving faster and farther than we anticipated."

Lena and Alex joined them at the map, their eyes scanning the lines and markings. "If they've reached the Faroe Islands, they're capable of striking almost anywhere in Europe," Lena said, her voice filled with concern.

"We need to alert the authorities in potential target areas," Alex added. "And we have to figure out their next move."

Commander Davis turned to Alina. "Send out an urgent communiqué to all relevant parties. They need to be prepared for anything."

Alina nodded and hurried back to the communications room. The rest of the team gathered around the map, the reality of the situation sinking in. The U-boat's actions were becoming bolder and more unpredictable, and they were running out of time to stop it.

"We need to find a way to anticipate their moves," Lena said, her mind racing. "There has to be a pattern, something we're missing. Alex nodded, his determination matching hers.

As the team delved back into their work with renewed urgency, the sense of boredom and unease was replaced by a palpable tension. The stakes had never been higher, and every moment counted. They were in a race against time, and failure was not an option.

**

Captain Bauer looked over the non-food items on display in the officer's dining area. He could barely understand the headlines of various newspapers and magazines and asked for Ingrid to be brought to him. Hans, standing at attention nearby, nodded and left the room to fetch her.

Ingrid was escorted again by Hans through the narrow corridors of the U-boat. As they approached the officer's dining area, she felt a mixture of curiosity and apprehension. The room was starkly lit, and her eyes were immediately drawn to the two computers sitting on the table amidst the scattered newspapers and magazines.

Her gaze lingered on the machines for a moment before she turned to face Captain Bauer, who was watching her intently. He had noticed her interest.

"Would you like some coffee?" he asked.

"Yes, that would be nice."

The Captain grabbed a coffee cup and poured her a cup, placing it on the table near the items.

"Fraulein, I see these devices have caught your attention. Can you translate the headlines for me?" Bauer asked, gesturing towards the array of newspapers and magazines.

Ingrid nodded, stepping closer to the table and sitting down. She picked up one of the newspapers, scanning the bold headlines quickly. "This one talks about a major political scandal. It seems a prominent government official was caught embezzling funds."

Bauer's expression remained impassive, but he listened closely as she continued.

"Another headline here mentions a breakthrough in medical research—something about a new vaccine that's showing promising results in trials."

She moved on to a magazine, flipping through the pages. "This magazine has an article on recent advancements in artificial intelligence. It highlights how artificial intelligence is becoming integral in various fields, from science to everyday life."

Bauer's eyes flicked to the two computers again, clearly intrigued. "And these machines, what are they?" he asked, his tone skeptical.

"They're computers," Ingrid explained, her voice steadying. "They can store and process vast amounts of information. Much more than any other device you might have on board."

"So, these machines are like our Enigma machines?"

"Well, not really. Your Enigma machine is really just a device to alter message and put them into code. A computer is capable to search for vast amounts of information. It's hard for me to really explain."

Bauer's skepticism was evident, but he was intrigued. "Can you open one of them and show me?"

Ingrid nodded and powered up one of the first computers. As it booted up, a login screen appeared. She tried a few common passwords, but each attempt was met with rejection. "Its password protected," she said, glancing at Bauer. "Without the correct password, I can't access the information inside."

"What is this thing called password?"

Ingrid sighs. "It is like a secret word that must be entered into the computer correctly before a person can use it."

Bauer frowned, clearly displeased. "Try the other one."

Ingrid moved to the second computer, feeling a surge of hope as it powered on without requiring a password. The desktop loaded, and she quickly attempted to navigate to her email, only to realize the computer had no way to connect to a network.

Her heart sank as she looked at the screen, knowing that without an internet connection, she couldn't send a message. She glanced at Captain Bauer, who was watching her intently, suspicion etched on his face.

"What's the matter?" he asked, noticing her hesitation.

"The computer needs to connect to a network to send emails or access any external information," Ingrid explained reluctantly.

Bauer's frown deepened. "What do you mean, 'connect to a network'?"

Ingrid took a deep breath, trying to find the simplest way to explain. "These computers can communicate with other computers through something called the Internet. It allows them to send and receive information from anywhere in the world. But without this connection, the computer can't communicate externally."

Bauer's eyes narrowed in confusion and skepticism. "So, it's useless to us then?"

"Not entirely," Ingrid replied, trying to think quickly. "There could be valuable information stored locally on the hard drive—documents, records, files, anything that might help us understand more about recent events or technological advancements."

Bauer seemed to consider this for a moment. "Fine. Search through the files and see what you can find. But remember, I am watching you."

Ingrid nodded and began to explore the computer's contents. She navigated through various folders, opening documents and scanning their contents. Most were mundane files, but she knew she had to keep looking.

As she worked, Bauer's eyes remained fixed on her, ensuring she didn't try anything suspicious. After several minutes, Ingrid found a document titled "Current Affairs Overview." She opened it and began to read aloud.

"This document discusses recent political changes in various countries, technological advancements, and economic forecasts," she explained. "There's a section here on a new vaccine showing promising results in clinical trials."

Bauer listened intently, his interest piqued. "Anything else?"

"Yes," Ingrid continued, flipping through more pages. "There's also information on major political scandals and some insights into new computer technologies that are being developed."

Bauer nodded, somewhat satisfied. "Good. Keep searching. We need all the information we can get."

Ingrid continued her search, her mind racing. She knew she had to find something useful quickly, both to satisfy Bauer and to keep herself safe. But without an internet connection, her options were limited.

Hans, standing guard nearby, watched with a mix of curiosity and wariness. Ingrid could sense his unease, and she hoped it might work to her advantage later. For now, she had to focus on the task at hand and find any valuable information hidden within the computer's files.

CHAPTER 27

Starting to become frustrated, Bauer asked Ingrid to find information about the weaponry that Russia, Great Britain, and the United States have access to. His patience was wearing thin, and his voice carried an edge of irritation.

"I'm sorry, Captain, but as I tried to explain, unless we can connect to the Internet, I cannot access that information," Ingrid said, her voice steady but tense.

Bauer quickly stood up, his expression darkening, and Ingrid thought she was about to get hit again. She flinched instinctively, her eyes wide with fear.

"Captain," she said quickly, trying to calm him, "I can give you an overview of what I know about the various weapons other nations have access to if that is what you want."

Bauer's interest was piqued. He paused, then slowly sat back down, his eyes never leaving hers. "Go on," he said, his voice calm but authoritative.

Ingrid took a deep breath, gathering her thoughts. She knew that the information she was about to share was sensitive, but it was the only way to keep Bauer from losing his temper.

"Alright," she began, "let's start with the United States. They have a range of advanced weaponry, including stealth aircraft like the F-22 Raptor and the F-35 Lightning II. These jets are nearly invisible to radar and can strike targets with pinpoint accuracy."

She glanced at Bauer to gauge his reaction. He was listening intently, his eyes narrowed in concentration.

"The U.S. has a powerful naval fleet, including aircraft carriers and nuclear submarines. Their submarines are armed with Trident II missiles, which can carry multiple nuclear warheads. They have advanced missile defense systems like the Aegis Ballistic Missile Defense System, designed to intercept and destroy incoming missiles."

Bauer nodded, indicating for her to continue.

"Great Britain has similar capabilities, though on a smaller scale. They have the Astute-class submarines, which are among the most advanced in the world. Their air force operates the Eurofighter Typhoon, a highly maneuverable aircraft equipped with advanced weaponry. Additionally, the British Army uses the Challenger 2 tank, known for its exceptional armor and firepower."

Ingrid paused for a moment, collecting her thoughts before moving on to the next country.

"Russia, on the other hand, has been investing heavily in modernizing its military. They have the Su-57 stealth fighter jets, which are designed to compete with the F-22 and F-35. Their missile technology is also quite advanced, with weapons like the S-400 and S-500 air defense systems capable of targeting aircraft and missiles at long ranges."

Bauer leaned back, absorbing the information. "And what about nuclear capabilities?" he asked, his tone more curious than demanding.

"Both the United States and Russia have extensive nuclear arsenals," Ingrid explained. "The U.S. maintains a triad of land-based missiles, submarine-launched missiles, and strategic bombers. Russia has a similar setup, with a variety of intercontinental ballistic missiles (ICBMs), submarine-launched ballistic missiles (SLBMs), and strategic bombers like the Tu-160."

Bauer nodded thoughtfully. "And Great Britain?"

"They have a smaller nuclear arsenal, but it's still significant," Ingrid replied. "Their main deterrent is the Vanguard-class submarines, each carrying Trident II missiles. These submarines ensure that Britain has a continuous at-sea deterrent."

The room fell silent as Bauer processed the information. Ingrid watched him carefully, hoping that her knowledge had satisfied his curiosity and calmed his frustration.

"You've been very informative, Fraulein," Bauer said finally, his tone more measured. "This information will be useful. You may go."

Hans stepped forward to escort Ingrid back to her quarters. As they walked down the corridor, Ingrid felt a mixture of relief and lingering fear. She had bought herself some time, but she knew that her situation was still precarious.

"Hans. Do you think I can get some food?"

"I will check with the captain. I can smell that the cook is making something."

Back in her quarters, Ingrid's mind raced. She had given Bauer a lot of valuable information, but she knew it was only a matter of time before he demanded more. She had to stay sharp and find a way to turn the situation to her advantage.

**

Commander Davis placed his coffee cup on the map reading table, a deep frown etched on his face. The steaming mug left a small ring of condensation on the surface, but he paid it no mind. He was joined by Chief Mercer, who also looked perplexed as he studied the spread of charts and intelligence reports.

"I don't understand why the U-boat headed towards Denmark. It altered its course away from Great Britain," Davis said, shaking his head in confusion.

Chief Mercer rubbed his chin thoughtfully, his eyes scanning the map. "It doesn't make much sense, sir. Denmark doesn't have any significant naval bases or strategic targets compared to Britain. Maybe they're trying to throw us off their trail or, since it was a grocery store they hit. Perhaps it simply was an attempt to restock their supplies."

Davis sighed and took a sip of his coffee, the bitter taste doing little to ease his frustration. "That's possible, Chief, but it feels like a risky move. They're using up precious fuel and resources to make these sudden course changes."

Chief Mercer nodded in agreement. "True, and each deviation from their expected path increases the chance of detection. They must have a specific reason for this detour."

Davis leaned over the map, tracing the U-boat's journey with his finger. "Let's consider their possible motivations. What could they have been after in Denmark?"

Mercer studied the map alongside Davis, his brow furrowed in concentration. "Well, there are several small islands in the Faroe Islands region. They might have been looking for a secluded place to restock supplies or repair damages without drawing too much attention."

Davis tapped a small dot on the map, representing one of the islands. "That's a good point. The Faroe Islands would have offered them a relatively quiet and isolated location for them to regroup. But that still doesn't explain the sudden urgency."

Chief Mercer leaned back, crossing his arms. "Perhaps they received new orders or intercepted some intelligence that made them change their plans. We did not have time to inspect their technology. If they're trying to avoid detection, they might have gotten wind of our patrol routes and adjusted accordingly."

Davis nodded slowly, considering the possibility. "That could be it. If they've intercepted our communications, they might be one step ahead of us. We need to be more cautious and unpredictable in our movements."

Mercer pointed to another area on the map. "There's also the chance they're attempting to rendezvous with another vessel or a covert supply ship. These waters are vast, and if they have allies, this might be the meeting point. Sadly, we both know that there are a lot of Nazi supporters out there even today."

Davis's eyes narrowed as he absorbed this new angle. "If that's the case, we need to disrupt their plans and cut off any potential support. We'll increase our patrols in this region and monitor for any unusual activity. Notify our reconnaissance teams to be on high alert."

Chief Mercer nodded briskly. "Understood, Commander. We'll tighten our net around the Faroe Islands and see if we can flush them out."

Davis sighed again, feeling a weight lift slightly off his shoulders. "And let's consider any civilian reports or sightings. Sometimes fishermen or local residents might notice something unusual. We need all the intel we can get."

Mercer added, "I'll also liaise with our allies in the area. They might have additional resources or information that could help us narrow down the U-boat's intentions."

Davis gave a resolute nod. "Good thinking. This U-boat has eluded us long enough. We need to anticipate their moves and stay one step ahead."

As Chief Mercer moved to carry out his orders, Davis took another sip of his coffee, his mind racing with strategies. The game of cat and mouse with the U-boat was intensifying, and every decision could mean the difference between success and failure. The stakes were higher than ever, and Davis knew they had to be vigilant and strategic to outmaneuver their elusive enemy.

CHAPTER 28

The atmosphere inside the U-boat was tense but focused as Captain Bauer moved through the narrow corridors. The routine of the day was abruptly interrupted when the sonar operator's voice crackled over the intercom.

"Captain Bauer, wir haben ein Schiff in der Nähe entdeckt," the operator reported, a note of urgency in his voice. [Captain Bauer, we've detected a ship in the vicinity.]

Bauer's eyes narrowed. "Periskop hoch," he ordered, making his way to the control room. [Up periscope.] The crew moved with practiced efficiency, each man at his station, ready for action.

The periscope emerged silently above the surface of the water, and Bauer peered through the lens. The gray expanse of the ocean came into focus, and in the distance, a ship appeared. His breath caught slightly as he recognized the markings. It was a Russian freighter, moving steadily across the water.

"Russischer Frachter gesichtet," Bauer announced, his voice carrying a mix of excitement and determination. [Russian freighter spotted.] "Bereit zum Angriff." [Prepare for the hunt.]

The crew sprang into action, the atmosphere in the U-boat electric with anticipation. Orders were barked, and the men moved quickly to ready the torpedoes. Bauer continued to watch the freighter through the periscope, his mind racing with tactical decisions.

"Torpedos auf Abschussposition bringen," he commanded, his tone calm but authoritative. [Set torpedoes to firing position.] The U-boat glided silently beneath the waves, positioning itself for the perfect strike.

The tension was palpable as the crew waited for Bauer's signal. He took a deep breath, his eyes never leaving the freighter. "Feuer Torpedos!" he ordered, his voice ringing out with finality. [Fire torpedoes!]

The U-boat shuddered slightly as the torpedoes were launched, streaking through the water towards their target. The seconds stretched into eternity as the crew watched the sonar screen, tracking the torpedoes' progress.

Then, with a thunderous explosion, the torpedoes struck the freighter. A cheer went up from the crew as they watched through the periscope. The ship was engulfed in flames, smoke billowing into the sky as it began to sink beneath the waves.

"Volltreffer!" the sonar operator confirmed, his voice filled with excitement. [Direct hit!]

Bauer allowed himself a small, satisfied smile. "Gut gemacht, Männer. Wir haben heute ein bedeutendes Ziel erreicht." [Well done, men. We've taken down a significant target today.]

The crew's enthusiasm was infectious, and the U-boat was filled with a sense of triumph. They had successfully hunted and sunk the freighter, a testament to their skill and precision.

As the freighter disappeared beneath the waves, Bauer lowered the periscope and turned to his crew. "Wir bleiben wachsam. Es könnten noch weitere Schiffe in der Nähe sein. Bleibt in Deckung und bereitet euch auf weitere Einsätze vor." [We stay vigilant. There may be more ships in the area. Maintain our stealth and prepare for any further engagements.]

Suddenly, the sonar operator's voice cut through the room again, this time with heightened urgency. "Captain, wir haben mehrere Sonarsignale in unserer Nähe entdeckt. Es könnten feindliche Schiffe sein." [Captain, we've detected multiple sonar signals nearby. They could be enemy ships.]

Bauer's face hardened. "Alle Mann an ihre Stationen. Sofort Kurs ändern!" [All men to their stations. Change course immediately!]

He turned to the navigation officer. "Nehmen Sie eine Zickzackroute und tauchen Sie tiefer. Wir müssen aus ihrem Suchbereich verschwinden." [Take a zigzag course and dive deeper. We need to get out of their search area.]

The U-boat crew sprang into action, the earlier triumph giving way to a sense of urgent efficiency. The engines roared softly as the submarine altered its course, plunging deeper into the dark waters. The hull creaked under the increased pressure, but the U-boat moved smoothly, evading potential detection.

"Sonartarnung aktivieren," Bauer commanded, watching the sonar screen intently. [Activate sonar decoys.]

Small devices were released from the submarine, designed to emit signals that would confuse any pursuing ships.

The tension was thick as the crew held their breaths, waiting to see if their maneuvers would succeed. The sonar screen showed the decoy signals spreading out, and slowly, the enemy signals began to disperse, moving away from their true position.

"Es funktioniert," the sonar operator whispered. [It's working.]

Bauer nodded, his expression one of steely determination. "Gut gemacht. Jetzt halten Sie den Kurs und die Tiefe. Wir müssen außer Reichweite bleiben." [Well done. Now maintain course and depth. We need to stay out of range.]

The U-boat continued on its new course, slipping further into the depths and away from the prying eyes of enemy ships. The crew gradually relaxed, though their vigilance never waned. They had successfully evaded detection, but the constant threat of discovery kept them on edge.

Bauer felt a surge of pride in his crew. They had proven themselves once again, and their unity and determination were unwavering. He knew they would face more challenges ahead, but with each victory, they grew stronger.

As the U-boat settled into its new course, the crew returned to their routines, their confidence bolstered by their recent triumph. The game of cat and mouse continued, and Bauer was determined to stay one step ahead of their enemies.

**

The boredom in the research center was broken when Alina announced that she had just received a message from the State Department. "A Russian freighter was torpedoed and sunk just south of its last known position of the U-boat," she said, her voice cutting through the stagnant air like a knife.

Commander Davis placed his coffee cup on the map reading table, his mind racing as the information sank in. He instantly realized that this had to be the work of the elusive U-boat they had been tracking. His heart pounded as he quickly checked the maps, tracing the erratic path of the submarine.

"I don't see any pattern to her course," he muttered, frustration clear in his voice. His eyes darted across the spread of charts, searching for any clue that might reveal the U-boat's intentions.

Chief Mercer leaned in, scrutinizing the maps alongside Davis. "You're right, sir. It's like they're deliberately avoiding a set pattern to throw us off."

The other officers gathered around, their expressions mirroring the tension and urgency of the situation. They nodded in agreement, their collective frustration palpable.

"It's almost as if they're playing a game of cat and mouse with us," one of the younger lieutenants remarked, his voice tinged with unease.

Davis exhaled sharply, running a hand through his hair. "They're making it difficult to predict their next move. We need to think like them, anticipate their strategies."

Chief Mercer tapped a point on the map, his finger moving along the possible routes. "If they're trying to evade us, they might be heading for less monitored waters. We need to cover all potential paths they could take."

Davis nodded, a determined glint in his eyes. "We need to be one step ahead. Inform all patrols and reconnaissance teams to expand their search areas. We can't let this U-boat slip through our fingers."

The officers dispersed to carry out Davis's orders, the room buzzing with renewed urgency. As Davis and Chief Mercer continued to study the maps, the weight of the responsibility pressed down on them. They knew the stakes were high, and the elusive U-boat had to be stopped before it could cause more havoc.

"We need to think strategically," Davis said, his voice resolute. "Let's predict their next possible move and set up an ambush. We'll use their unpredictability against them."

Chief Mercer agreed, his respect for Davis's leadership growing. "Yes, sir. We'll outmaneuver them this time."

The hunt was back on, and the team was more determined than ever. With every passing minute, the tension mounted, but so did their resolve. The elusive U-boat had met its match, and Davis was prepared to do whatever it took to bring it to heel.

CHAPTER 29

As the night drew on, Alex and Lena lingered in the dining area, finishing off the last of their dinner. The conversation had been pleasant, but the day's events had left them both weary. They decided to turn in for the night.

"I'm going to take a shower before bed," Lena mentioned as they rose from the table. "I'll meet you in your room afterward."

Alex nodded. "Sounds good. Don't take too long," he teased with a smile.

They parted ways, Lena heading towards her room. The dimly lit hallway was quiet, save for the soft padding of her footsteps on the carpet. As she neared her door, a faint sound caught her attention—a low, rhythmic buzzing.

Pausing, Lena realized the sound was coming from Ingrid's room. She approached the door, which was slightly ajar, and the buzzing grew louder. It was Ingrid's cellphone ringing. Lena hesitated, but curiosity got the better of her. She pushed the door open gently and stepped inside.

The room was dim, shadows playing across the walls from the small bedside lamp. Ingrid was nowhere to be seen, but her phone lay on the dresser, vibrating insistently. Lena glanced around, feeling a strange sense of intrusion, but something compelled her to pick up the phone.

"Hello?" she said cautiously.

There was a brief silence, then a voice, deep and resonant with a thick Russian accent, crackled through the speaker. "Report."

Lena's heart skipped a beat. She stood frozen, the word echoing in her mind. The voice on the other end waited, the silence between them growing heavier by the second.

"Who is this?" she finally managed to whisper, but the call had already ended.

She stared at the phone, her thoughts racing. The word "report" hung in the air like a dark cloud. Could Ingrid be a Russian agent? The idea seemed absurd, yet the evidence was there, clear and undeniable. Her focus on the cryonic section of the U-boat the interest with the nuclear reactor.

Lena's mind swirled with suspicion and fear as she quickly put the phone back where she found it and slipped out of the room, closing the door quietly behind her.

After her shower, she made her way to Alex's room, her thoughts were in turmoil. She needed to tell him what had happened, but how could she explain it without sounding paranoid? Taking a deep breath, she knocked on his door, her hand trembling slightly.

Alex opened the door, his expression softening when he saw her. "Hey, you okay?"

Lena stepped inside, glancing over her shoulder as if expecting someone to be following her. "Alex, we need to talk," she said, her voice barely above a whisper. "Something's not right about Ingrid."

Lena's heart pounded as she relayed the encounter to Alex. His expression shifted from concern to focused intensity as he listened to her account of the phone call.

"A Russian accent? And he said 'report'? That's... troubling," Alex said, rubbing his chin thoughtfully.

"I know it sounds crazy, but what if Ingrid is a Russian agent?" Lena whispered, her eyes wide with a mixture of fear and determination. "We need to find out more."

Alex nodded. "Let's check her room, but we need to be discreet. If she is an agent, we can't let her know we're onto her once we find her."

They waited until the hallway was completely quiet, the only sound the distant crashing of waves against the shore. Then, they slipped out of Alex's room and crept down the hallway to Ingrid's door.

Lena's pulse raced as she slowly turned the doorknob, praying it wouldn't creak.

Inside, the room was as dimly lit as before. They moved quickly but quietly, searching for any clues that could confirm their suspicions. Lena opened the drawer of the bedside table and found a notebook filled with hastily scribbled notes. She flipped through the pages, her eyes widening at its content.

"Alex, look at this," she whispered, handing the notebook to him. "These are coded messages. They must be for her handler."

Alex scanned the notes, his brow furrowing. "This is definitely suspicious. We need to document this and keep it safe, plus show it to Commander Davis."

They continued their search, finding more incriminating evidence—maps with marked locations, a list of dates and times that coincided with local events, and a small stash of foreign currency. Each discovery added to the mounting evidence against Ingrid.

"We should take pictures of all this," Alex suggested. "We need proof if we're going to report her."

Lena nodded and pulled out her phone, quickly snapping pictures of the notes and other items. As they worked, a sense of urgency gripped them. They needed to get out of the room before Ingrid returned.

Suddenly, the sound of footsteps echoed in the hallway. Lena's heart skipped a beat. "She's coming back!" she whispered urgently.

"She can't be. She's on the U-boat."

"Your right. What the hell am I thinking?"

They hurriedly put everything back in its place and slipped out of the room, closing the door quietly behind them. They dashed back to Alex's room, breathing heavily as they tried to calm their racing hearts.

"That was close," Alex said, wiping sweat from his forehead. "But we have what we need."

As they sat down to review the pictures and notes they had gathered, a chilling realization settled over them. They were now part of a much larger and more dangerous game than they had ever anticipated.

"Let's get some sleep and share our findings with the Commander," Lena said.

"I have a better idea," Alex said as he reached out and pulled Lena towards him.

CHAPTER 30

Captain Bauer leaned over the large table in the command room of U-boat 420, his eyes intently scanning the maps and charts spread out before him. The dim red light cast an eerie glow, reflecting off the brass instruments and the edges of the meticulously drawn lines indicating various courses and positions.

The hum of the engines and the creaking of the submarine as it cut through the deep waters of the Atlantic were the only sounds, a constant reminder of the hostile environment they navigated. Bauer's brow furrowed as he traced a route with his finger, considering the potential threats and opportunities that lay ahead.

"Helmsman," Bauer called, his voice steady and authoritative.

The helmsman, a young but experienced sailor named Dietrich, snapped to attention. "Ja, Herr Kapitän?"

"Kurs ändern," Bauer commanded, his voice resonating with the weight of his decision. "Bringen Sie uns auf Kurs zwei-drei-null Grad. Wir werden nach Großbritannien steuern." ("Change course. Bring us to heading 230 degrees. We are heading towards Great Britain.")

"Jawohl, Herr Kapitän," Dietrich responded, immediately turning to adjust the controls. The submarine began its slow, deliberate turn to the new heading, the creaking of the hull intensifying slightly as it responded to the change in direction.

Bauer watched the compass, ensuring the course was true. He knew that their mission was entering a critical phase. The intelligence they had gathered pointed to a significant convoy that would be passing through the waters off the coast of Great Britain. Intercepting it could deal a substantial blow to the enemy's supply lines.

As he returned to the command room, Bauer could feel the weight of responsibility on his shoulders. Every decision he made could mean the difference between life and death for his crew, and the success or failure of their mission. He glanced at his watch. Time was of the essence.

"All stations, we will continue with silent running," Bauer ordered. "We need to remain undetected until we are in position. We are now heading for our first primary target, England. In one hour, if no aircrafts or surface vessels are seen, we will surface briefly to fill our boat with fresh air. The Fuhrer has provided us with a super sub and so far, our enemies are not a match for us."

The crew moved with practiced efficiency, their faces set with determination. They knew the risks, but they also knew the importance of their mission. Bauer took a deep breath and looked around at his men. "We have a long journey ahead, but I have faith in each and every one of you. Stay sharp, and we'll come through this. Heil Hitler."

The submarine continued its course, the dark waters of the Atlantic closing around it like a shroud. The men of U-boat 420 braced themselves for the challenges that lay ahead, steeling their nerves for the encounters yet to come.

Captain Bauer returned to his maps, his mind already several steps ahead, planning and anticipating the moves they would need to make. The sea was an unforgiving adversary, but Bauer was determined to lead his crew to victory, no matter the cost.

**

Neither Lena nor Alex could really sleep, and it wasn't due to a lack of intimacy the night before. Instead, their minds raced, unable to shut off as they grappled with the gravity of the allegations they were prepared to share with Commander Davis and, subsequently, the Norwegian government.

The two walked into the dining area together, bypassing the coffee station and heading straight to the table where Chief and Commander Davis were enjoying their breakfast. "Good morning, Commander, Chief," Alex began. "We have something to share with you both."

The Chief and Commander Davis glanced at each other before shifting to make space. Lena took a seat next to the Chief while Alex sat beside the Commander.

"Last night, on my way to my room, I heard a noise coming from Ingrid's room," Lena started. "When I went in, I saw it was her cellphone ringing, so I answered it. On the other end was a man with a Russian accent. As soon as he realized it wasn't Ingrid, he hung up."

Commander Davis exchanged a serious look with the Chief, both sensing that what Lena and Alex had to share next wouldn't be good news.

"I immediately shared this with Alex," Lena continued. "We both agreed it was necessary to search her room. We found several incriminating documents. Here are some pictures of what we discovered. It looks like Ingrid has been gathering information to pass on to the Russian government."

Lena slid her cellphone across the table to the Commander and Chief. As they scanned through the images of coded messages, marked maps, and foreign currency, their expressions grew increasingly grim.

"This information must remain strictly between the four of us until I consult with the State Department to determine the appropriate course of action. We're dealing with a situation that exceeds our authority. The presence of a rogue German U-boat equipped with technology that matches, if not surpasses, our own is a severe threat. In my report, I will strongly recommend that global leaders be urgently informed. The stakes are incredibly high—if this U-boat launches an attack on any nation without prior warning, we will be held accountable for our failure to alert them. The potential for catastrophic consequences demands our utmost discretion and swift action."

**

After an hour passed, Hans approached Captain Bauer to inform him that Ingrid had not received any food. Bauer nodded, instructing him to prepare a plate and bring some water. As Hans walked toward Ingrid's room, she strategized her next psychological move.

"I brought you food," Hans said as he entered.

"Thank God, I was starving," Ingrid replied, purposefully leaning forward to give Hans a clear view of her cleavage. He started to leave after placing the food and drink on the table.

"Hans, please stay. I'm really scared and I feel much better when you are with me." Hans nodded and took a seat opposite her. She put some food in her mouth and chewed slowly.

"Doesn't taste good?" Hans asked. "At times, our cook's meals are wunderbar, but occasionally it tastes like..."

"Shit," Ingrid interjected.

"Yes, shit," Hans said, smiling.

Ingrid leaned in closer, her voice dropping to a conspiratorial whisper. "Hans, there's something I need to tell you. Something that I've told the Captain, but he hasn't shared with your crewmates."

Hans raised an eyebrow, curiosity piqued. "What is it?"

Ingrid glanced around as if to ensure no one else could hear. "Hitler is dead," she said, her voice barely above a whisper. "He committed suicide, and Germany lost the war. It was divided into sections by the Allies. Originally, it was split into four sections, but now it is united into a republic."

Hans's eyes widened in shock, disbelief evident on his face. "That can't be true," he stammered. "How could you know this?"

"Hans, do you know what year it is now?" Ingrid asked. Not expecting an answer, she continued, "The year is 2024. The Germany you knew and loved ended in 1945."

Hans sat back, the weight of the information sinking in. If this were true, it changed everything.

His mind raced with questions and doubts, but the possibility was too staggering to ignore.

After a few moments of stunned silence, Hans stood up. “I need to inform the Captain,” he said, his voice shaky. “If what you say is true, he needs to know.”

“Hans, you cannot tell the Captain I told you. He will beat me or even kill me. You must promise to keep it to yourself.” Hans remained standing, his thoughts swirling. Finally, without saying anything, he left the room.

Ingrid watched him leave, a satisfied smile playing on her lips. Her plan was unfolding perfectly.

CHAPTER 31

"Where the hell is she?" Commander Davis muttered in frustration to no one in particular. "Three P-3 Orions and still no sight of her. If she had a malfunction, she could be at the bottom of the ocean and we wouldn't know it."

"All we can do now is wait," the Chief responded. "From her last known position, she could have gone north, south, east, or west. Then again, you might be right—she could have sunk again."

**

"Captain, Sonar." ("Kapitän, Sonar.")

"This is the Captain. What do you have?" ("Hier spricht der Kapitän. Was haben Sie?")

"Another ship, 200 meters off our bow." ("Ein weiteres Schiff, 200 Meter vor unserem Bug.")

"Helmsman, bring her to periscope depth." ("Steuermann, bringen Sie sie auf Sehrohrtiefe.")

"Aye, Captain." ("Ja, Kapitän.")

The helmsman quickly adjusted the controls, and the submarine began its slow ascent to periscope depth. The tension in the control room was palpable as the crew anticipated what they might find.

"Periscope depth achieved, Captain," the helmsman reported. ("Sehrohrtiefe erreicht, Kapitän.")

Captain Bauer nodded and moved to the periscope, raising it and peering through the lenses. The dim light of the control room contrasted sharply with the bright daylight above the surface, making the transition jarring.

Bauer focused on the horizon, scanning for any signs of the ship that sonar had detected. "I see it. It looks like a destroyer, but a type I have never seen before. Load torpedoes one and two. ("Ich sehe es. Es ist ein Handelsschiff, das nach Nordosten fährt.")

"Maintain periscope depth and keep us at a safe distance," Bauer ordered. ("Halten Sie die Sehrohrtiefe und halten Sie uns auf sicherer Entfernung.")

"Aye, Captain." ("Ja, Kapitän.")

The submarine held its position, silently gliding through the water as they monitored the merchant vessel. The crew remained alert, ready for any command from Bauer as they awaited the next move.

"Target in range, Captain," the XO said. ("Ziel in Reichweite, Kapitän," sagte der XO.)

"Up periscope," Bauer ordered. ("Periskop hoch," befahl Bauer.)

“Periscope depth, Captain,” the XO advised. (“Sehrohrtiefe erreicht, Kapitän,” meldete der XO.) Bauer once again recorded the U-boat’s range to the target.

“Fire one! Fire two!” Bauer commanded. (“Feuer eins! Feuer zwei!” befahl Bauer.)

A rush of sound echoed through the U-boat as the torpedoes were launched. The crew strained their hearing, hoping to catch the sound of an impact. They were not disappointed.

The XO looked at his stopwatch. “First torpedo should hit now.” (“Der erste Torpedo sollte jetzt treffen.”) A loud explosion reverberated through the submarine, followed by cheers from the crew.

“The second, now!” he announced, just as another explosion rocked the vessel. (“Der zweite, jetzt!” verkündete er, als eine weitere Explosion das Schiff erschütterte.)

The crew erupted in celebration, their tension melting away in the wake of their successful attack. Bauer allowed himself a brief moment of satisfaction before refocusing on the task at hand.

“Maintain current depth and course,” he ordered. (“Halten Sie aktuelle Tiefe und Kurs,” befahl er.)

“Aye, Captain.” (“Ja, Kapitän.”)

The U-boat continued its silent glide through the water, the crew’s spirits lifted by their recent victory. But Bauer knew that vigilance was crucial; their enemies would soon be on high alert, and the next encounter could be even more dangerous.

The XO looked at Bauer. "The Führer would be proud of our accomplishments so far, Captain." ("Der Führer wäre stolz auf unsere bisherigen Erfolge, Kapitän.")

Bauer nodded. "By this time tomorrow, after we launch the rocket into the center of London, the world powers will stop at nothing to send us to the bottom of the sea. And this time, we won't be frozen." ("Um diese Zeit morgen, nachdem wir die Rakete ins Zentrum von Moskau abgefeuert haben, werden die Weltmächte nichts unversucht lassen, um uns auf den Meeresgrund zu schicken. Und dieses Mal werden wir nicht eingefroren sein.")

"Should I maintain our present course?" the XO asked. ("Soll ich unseren jetzigen Kurs beibehalten?")

"Yes," Bauer confirmed. "Before we reach the ideal range to launch, we must surface and open the housing containing the rocket. That will be when we are the most vulnerable. It will be critical to launch quickly and then dive to the safety of the ocean depths while setting a course for the coast of northern Russia.

The weight of the mission hung heavy in the control room, each crew member silently acknowledging the high stakes. They knew the risks involved; one mistake could lead to their demise, but their commitment to the mission was unwavering.

After a short break with his officers, Bauer once again, ordered the helmsman to come to periscope depth. Once achieve he checked the surface for any enemy ships. Finding it clear, he gave the order to surface.

"Prepare the crew for surfacing," Bauer ordered. "Ensure all stations are ready and the rocket housing is secure." ("Bereiten Sie die Besatzung auf das Auftauchen vor," befahl Bauer. "Stellen Sie sicher, dass alle Stationen bereit sind und das Raketengehäuse gesichert ist.")

"Aye, Captain," the XO responded, moving swiftly to relay the orders. ("Ja, Kapitän," antwortete der XO und eilte davon, um die Befehle weiterzugeben.)

Bauer turned back to the periscope, watching the horizon with steely determination. The success of their mission depended on precise timing and flawless execution. He knew his crew was capable, but the pressure of their task was immense.

As the submarine glided through the dark waters, the tension among the crew was palpable. They moved with practiced efficiency, checking and double-checking their equipment, aware that any lapse could be fatal.

The submarine leveled off on the surface Bauer and the XO manned the conning tower. Both, using binoculars, searched the area and found it free of enemy vessels. "Prepare to open the rocket housing." ("Boot auftauchen. Bereiten Sie sich darauf vor, das Raketengehäuse zu öffnen.")

Soon the deck for the U-boat was filled with men removing a portion of the deck covering revealing the newest V-4 rocket of the former Third Reich. "Rocket housing is open and secure, Captain," the XO reported. ("Das Raketengehäuse ist geöffnet und gesichert, Kapitän," meldete der XO.)

"Captain, Helmsman. We are in range of the target." Bauer looked at his XO. "For the Fuhrer, for the Fatherland, and for our brothers who died gallantly in Stalingrad."

"Commence launch sequence," Bauer ordered. ("Startsequenz einleiten," befahl Bauer.)

The tension in the air was electric as the crew executed the final steps of their mission.The rocket ignited with a roar, propelling itself toward its target.

"Rocket away," the XO confirmed. ("Rakete gestartet," bestätigte der XO.)

Inside the confined and tense atmosphere of the U-boat, the crew felt the deep rumble as the V-4 rocket launched off the deck. The reverberation of the powerful thrust seemed to shake every bolt and rivet in the submarine. Commander Bauer and his Executive Officer, stationed at the periscope, strained to follow the rocket's trajectory through the narrow viewport. As the rocket ascended into the sky, leaving a trail of white smoke, a sense of anticipation gripped everyone on board.

Moments later, a brilliant flash lit up the distant horizon, followed by a thunderous roar that seemed to echo through the ocean itself. The shockwave reverberated back to the submarine, underscoring the immense power of the explosion. Bauer and his XO watched in awe as a massive mushroom cloud billowed upwards, darkening the sky and signifying the successful hit on their target. The destructive force of the blast was unmistakable, a grim confirmation of their mission's success. London was ablaze.

"Dive! Dive! Dive!" Bauer shouted, urgency in his voice. ("Tauchen! Tauchen! Tauchen!" rief Bauer, die Dringlichkeit in seiner Stimme.)

The U-boat plunged back into the depths, the crew holding their breath as they descended to safety. The ocean closed around them, providing the cover they needed to evade detection.

"Set course for northern Russia," Bauer commanded, his voice calm and resolute. ("Kurs auf die Vereinigten Staaten setzen," befahl Bauer, seine Stimme ruhig und entschlossen.)

As the U-boat settled into its new course, the crew allowed themselves a moment of relief. The most dangerous part of their mission was over, but the journey ahead was still fraught with peril.

Bauer stood tall in the control room, his mind already on the next steps. The world had changed, and they were at the center of a new and unpredictable conflict. But for now, they had survived, and their mission continued.

CHAPTER 32

"Commander," Alina called out, her voice trembling. "London has been attacked."

Television sets flickered to life, casting an eerie glow in the dimly lit room. The screens displayed scenes of unimaginable devastation. The heart of London lay in ruins, a smoldering wasteland where vibrant neighborhoods and iconic landmarks once stood. Buildings were reduced to twisted metal and crumbling concrete, while fires raged uncontrollably, casting a hellish red hue across the sky.

Thick plumes of black smoke spiraled upwards, blotting out the sun and leaving the city in a perpetual twilight. Streets were littered with debris, overturned vehicles, and the haunting silhouettes of what remained of everyday life.

As the horrifying images played out, the full extent of the nuclear blast's impact became painfully clear. The shockwave had flattened entire blocks, and the intense heat had melted glass and steel, leaving behind a nightmarish landscape. The once bustling metropolis was now a silent testament to the catastrophic power unleashed upon it. No one spoke.

Commander Davis's phone rang breaking the silence in the command center. "I understand, is all that anyone heard in the conversation coming from the Commander. "An emergency session of the United Nations has been called. The United States has directed it Atlantic submarine fleet into the north Atlantic.

**

The President was abruptly awakened from a deep sleep by the urgent knocking on his bedroom door. His heart raced as he glanced at the clock—2:43 AM. He had a sinking feeling that this was not a routine wake-up call. The knocking persisted, growing more insistent.

"Mr. President, we need you immediately," came the urgent voice of his Chief of Staff, Margaret.

The President quickly donned his robe and opened the door to find Margaret and several top advisors, their faces etched with concern. "What's happened?" he asked, his voice thick with sleep.

"Sir, there's been an attack," Margaret said, her voice trembling slightly. "A nuclear device has detonated in London. We believe it was launched from a rogue German U-boat."

The President's blood ran cold. "London? How bad is it? What do you mean a rogue German U-boat?"

Margaret nodded, handing him a secure phone. "We have confirmation from multiple sources. The devastation is total, sir. The casualty estimates are already in the hundreds of thousands, and they're rising. The city is in chaos."

The President took the phone and dialed the emergency number that connected him directly to the National Security Council's situation room. Within moments, he was patched through to the grim faces of his national security team, who were gathered around a large screen displaying live footage from London.

"Mr. President," said the Secretary of Defense, his voice steady but grim. "We're still assessing the full extent of the damage, but initial reports indicate a catastrophic loss of life and infrastructure. A V-4 rocket was launched from a German U-boat. We have its last known coordinates in the Barents Sea, but it's now submerged and on the move."

"A German U-boat? What the hell is a Nazi submarine active? How come I was not notified of this German U-boat? God damn it, I thought I got rid of the former liberals assholes in this office. Never mind. I will take care of that later."

The President's mind raced. "Have we notified our allies? What's our next move?"

"We've alerted NATO, the UN, and our key allies," the Secretary of State interjected. "There's an emergency session scheduled in less than an hour. The world is looking to us for a response."

"A lot good the damn UN will do. All they want is to collect more and more money from us and do nothing."

The President took a deep breath, trying to process the enormity of the situation. "We need to confirm the identity and location of that U-boat and ensure it cannot launch another attack. And we need to support the UK in their immediate recovery efforts. Have we put our forces on high alert?"

"Yes, sir," replied the Chairman of the Joint Chiefs. "All strategic forces are on high alert. We're ready to respond at a moment's notice."

The President nodded, his face set with determination. "Get me Prime Minister Harrington on the line. I need to speak with him personally."

Within moments, the secure line was connected to Downing Street. The President could hear the panic and controlled chaos in the background as Prime Minister Harrington came on the line.

"Mr. President," Harrington's voice was strained, barely masking the underlying horror. "London is for the most part, gone. It is a miracle that I am hear speaking with you. The devastation is beyond comprehension."

"Prime Minister, I'm deeply sorry for your loss. We stand with you. We'll do everything in our power to support you and bring those responsible to justice," the President assured him. "Our intelligence indicates a rogue German U-boat launched the attack. We're mobilizing our forces to track it down."

"Thank you," Harrington replied, his voice breaking. "We need all the help we can get. The people are terrified, and the situation is dire."

The President exchanged a few more words of solidarity before ending the call. He turned back to his advisors, his face resolute. "We have to neutralize that U-boat and prevent any further attacks. We must also coordinate a comprehensive international response. This is an act of war, and we must be prepared for the consequences."

The room fell silent as the weight of the President's words settled over them. The path ahead was fraught with peril, but the resolve in the room was unwavering. The President knew that the coming days would test their leadership and the resilience of the free world. But they had no choice—they had to face this threat head-on.

"Margaret, get me a briefing with the Joint Chiefs. I want every available resource focused on finding and neutralizing that U-boat. And prepare a statement for the nation. The American people need to know we're taking decisive action."

"Yes, Mr. President," Margaret responded, already moving to execute his orders.

The President glanced at the live footage of London once more, feeling the weight of the world's expectations on his shoulders. As he stepped into the situation room, he steeled himself for the battle ahead, knowing that the fate of countless lives depended on their actions in the coming hours and days.

"Also, I want the best historian we have here ASAP telling me about this U-boat. How in hell is a Nazi U-boat still working?"

CHAPTER 33

"Dr. Lawrence, Dr. Müller, Dr. Sousa, pack a bag. The four of us have been ordered to meet the President in D.C. Our plane leaves in one hour," Commander Davis commanded, his tone leaving no room for hesitation.

"Do we know for what purpose?" Alex Sousa inquired, glancing at Lena Lawrence and Dr. Müller, who shared the same look of curiosity and concern.

"Yes," Davis replied, his expression serious. "The President wants us to bring him up to speed regarding the U-boat. Believe it or not, the State Department has kept him in the dark about everything. I think heads will roll, but that's not our concern."

The seriousness of the situation settled over them like a heavy fog. Lena, still reeling from the earlier news about London, felt a knot tighten in her stomach. The implications of their mission were enormous. She quickly gathered her essential items, her mind racing with the possible outcomes of their meeting with the President.

The group moved with urgency, their footsteps echoing down the sterile corridors of the research facility. They were escorted to a waiting vehicle that would take them to the airstrip. The ride was silent, each of them lost in their thoughts, contemplating the magnitude of the crisis they were about to confront.

As they boarded the sleek, government-issued jet, Lena couldn't shake the image of the mushroom cloud over London from her mind. The devastation was a stark reminder of the destructive power they were dealing with. She glanced at her colleagues, all of whom seemed equally burdened by the weight of their mission.

The plane ascended swiftly, cutting through the night sky towards Washington, D.C. Inside, the atmosphere was tense, the hum of the engines providing a constant backdrop to their silent reflections. Commander Davis broke the silence, briefing them on what to expect once they landed.

"We'll be meeting the President and his top advisors in the Situation Room. It's imperative that we provide them with a comprehensive overview of the U-boat's capabilities and the threat it poses. This information is critical to formulating a response strategy."

Dr. Müller nodded, his face set in determination. "We'll give them everything they need. This situation has escalated beyond anything we could have anticipated."

Lena and Alex exchanged a glance, silently acknowledging the enormity of the task ahead. They knew that their expertise and insights would play a crucial role in shaping the response to this unprecedented threat.

As the plane began its descent into Washington, the city's lights twinkling below them, Lena took a deep breath, steeling herself for the confrontation to come. They had a responsibility not just to the President, but to the world, to ensure that the information they provided would help prevent further catastrophe.

Upon landing, they were whisked away to the White House, the gravity of their mission underscored by the solemn expressions of the officials who greeted them. The halls of power buzzed with a sense of urgency and tension, the usual bustle replaced by a focused intensity.

They were led directly to the Situation Room, where the President and his advisors were already assembled. The room was filled with the hum of conversation and the flicker of screens displaying real-time intelligence and satellite images.

"Thank you for coming," the President said, looking at the four individuals before him.

"Mr. President," Commander Davis began, "we're here to provide you with the full scope of the threat posed by the rogue German U-boat and its capabilities."

The President, his face lined with worry but resolute, nodded. "We need all the information you can provide. Lives are at stake, and we must act swiftly and decisively."

Lena stepped forward, her voice steady despite the whirlwind of emotions inside her. "The U-boat is equipped with advanced missile technology, capable of launching nuclear devices like the one that devastated London. We have reason to believe it is currently positioned off the coast of Northern Russia, and it poses a significant threat to any nation within its range."

As they detailed the U-boat's capabilities and the potential for further attacks, the room fell silent, the weight of their words hanging heavy in the air. The President listened intently, his advisors taking notes and asking pointed questions.

When they had finished, the President leaned forward, his expression grave but determined. "Thank you for your thorough briefing. We will take immediate action to track and neutralize this threat. Your expertise has been invaluable. I'm sorry, but I must request that you stay here in Washington until we can located and stop the U-boat. My Chief of Staff will arrange for a place for you to stay."

As they exited the Situation Room, the group felt a sense of solemn responsibility. They had done their part, providing the necessary information to those in power. Now, it was up to the leaders of the free world to take the decisive action needed to prevent further tragedy. The fate of countless lives depended on their swift and effective response.

**

As the President's wrapped up his meeting, the U-boat surfaced stealthily in the frigid waters of the Barents Sea, the shoreline of Northern Russia barely visible in the distance. The crew moved with practiced precision, their faces set in grim determination as they prepared for the second launch of a V-4 rocket. Below deck, the atmosphere was tense, every man acutely aware of the devastation they were about to unleash.

"Prepare for launch," Commander Bauer ordered, his voice steady but cold. The crew swiftly followed his commands, their movements synchronized as they readied the rocket.

Above deck, the massive missile stood poised against the icy sky, its sleek form a stark contrast to the desolate surroundings. The countdown began, each second ticking away with the weight of impending doom.

"Ten... nine... eight..." The voice over the intercom was clear and unwavering. As the final second approached, the rocket engines roared to life, the vessel vibrating with the immense power of the launch.

"Three... two... one... launch!"

The V-4 rocket shot off the deck with a thunderous roar, cutting through the air and disappearing into the cloudy sky. The crew watched its ascent, the trail of smoke a grim reminder of their mission's destructive force.

Minutes later, the horizon lit up with an intense flash, followed by a deafening explosion. The shockwave reached the U-boat, shaking it violently as the crew held on to whatever they could. Through the periscope, Bauer and his XO observed the horrifying aftermath. A colossal mushroom cloud rose ominously over the Russian coastline, a testament to the nuclear devastation that had just been unleashed.

The once-frozen landscape was now a scene of utter chaos and ruin. Buildings and structures near the impact site were obliterated, their remains scattered across the tundra. Fires blazed uncontrollably, their flames reflecting off the snow, creating an apocalyptic tableau. The force of the blast had leveled entire areas, leaving nothing but charred remnants and smoldering ashes in its wake.

As the U-boat descended back into the depths, the crew was left with the stark realization of the immense power they wielded and the catastrophic consequences of their actions.

Captain Bauer looked sternly at his XO. "No doubt we have this new world's attention. I just hope that we will have enough time to hit our main target. Set course for the eastern coast of America."

CHAPTER 34

In the dimly lit galley of the rogue German U-boat, the air was thick with the scent of diesel fuel and the lingering aroma of stewed vegetables. The ship's cook, a burly man with grease-stained hands, stirred a pot of soup, his thoughts far away from the chaos above the waves.

Hans, with a face etched in worry and resolve, entered the galley quietly. He glanced around, ensuring they were alone before approaching the cook.

"Gustav," Hans whispered, his voice barely audible over the hum of the engines. "We need to talk."

Gustav looked up, his brows furrowing. "What is it, Hans? You look like you've seen a ghost."

"It's worse than that," Hans said, his voice trembling. "I have to tell you something—something Ingrid told me when I brought her food, " He trailed off, the memory too painful to complete.

Gustav set the ladle down and motioned for Hans to sit. "Speak up, boy. What's on your mind?"

Hans leaned in closer, his voice dropping to a conspiratorial whisper. "It's about the Führer. About the end of the war. Everything we've been told is a lie."

The cook's eyes widened, but he remained silent, urging Hans to continue.

"Ingrid told me the truth," Hans said. "Our Fuhrer, Adolf Hitler is dead. He took his own life in his bunker as the Allies closed in. The Third Reich has fallen, Gustav. We're fighting for a ghost."

Gustav's face turned pale, the weight of Hans' words sinking in. "But the Reich's broadcasts… the victory messages…"

"All lies," Hans interrupted, his voice urgent. "Propaganda to keep us in line, to keep us fighting. But it's over. We're just pawns in a game that's already lost. And the worse news, is that we are in 2024, not 1945. The war has been over for decades."

Gustav sat back, his mind racing. "Why are you telling me this, Hans? What can we do?"

Hans glanced around nervously. "We have to survive, Gustav. We have to find a way out of this madness. If the others find out what we know, they'll think we're traitors."

The cook nodded slowly, his eyes narrowing in thought. "We'll have to be careful. We must keep it to ourselves and only share it with those we trust."

Hans nodded, relief washing over him. "Thank you, Gustav. I knew I could trust you."

As the two men sat in the quiet galley, the weight of their shared secret pressed heavily upon them. The truth was a dangerous burden, one that could cost them their lives if discovered. But it was also a beacon of hope, a sliver of light in the darkness that could guide them to a future beyond the ruins of the Third Reich.

**

The Situation Room was a hive of activity, filled with the murmurs of advisors and the glow of digital screens displaying real-time intelligence. The President, seated at the head of the long conference table, was deep in discussion with his top military and intelligence advisors about the V-4 rocket attack on London. The gravity of the situation was palpable.

Suddenly, the double doors of the room swung open, and the Chief of Staff, a tall man with a stern expression and a phone pressed against his ear, hurried in. He approached the President, who looked up with a frown.

"Mr. President, I need a moment," the Chief of Staff said, his voice urgent but controlled.

The President nodded, signaling a brief pause in the meeting. "What is it, David?" he asked, rising from his chair and stepping aside with his Chief of Staff.

David's face was grim as he spoke. "We've just received word that Moscow has been attacked. Reports are coming in of multiple explosions and widespread devastation. Preliminary intelligence suggests another V-4 rocket strike."

The President's eyes widened, and he took a deep breath, steadying himself. "My God," he muttered. "Get me Putin. Now."

David nodded and stepped away to arrange the call, while the President turned back to his advisors. "Ladies and gentlemen, it appears London wasn't the only target. Moscow has just been hit. We need to escalate our response and coordinate with our international partners immediately."

The room erupted into action as the President moved to the secure phone line. Within moments, the line connected, and he heard the unmistakable voice of President Vladimir Putin, strained with urgency.

"Mr. President," Putin began, his voice a mix of anger and anxiety. "I assume you've heard the news?"

"Yes, Vladimir, I have," the President replied. "This is an unprecedented crisis. We need to work together to address this threat. What can you tell me about the situation on the ground in Moscow?"

Putin's response was terse. "The damage is extensive. Several key areas of the city have been hit, including government buildings and military installations. We're still assessing the full extent, but the casualties are already staggering."

The President nodded, even though Putin couldn't see him. "We're mobilizing all available resources to track down the source of these attacks. We believe a rogue German U-boat is responsible. Our intelligence teams are working around the clock to locate and neutralize it. In the meantime, we need to strengthen our defenses and share any relevant intelligence."

"Agreed," Putin said, his tone softening slightly. "We'll do the same on our end. This threat concerns us all, and we must stand united."

"Thank you, Vladimir," the President said. "We'll keep the lines of communication open and coordinate our efforts closely. We can't afford any missteps."

As the call ended, the President turned back to his team, his expression resolute. "Ladies and gentlemen, our task just became more urgent. We have to find that U-boat and stop any further attacks. The world is counting on us."

With renewed determination, the room buzzed with focused energy, each person committed to their role in addressing the unfolding global crisis. The President knew the stakes had never been higher, and every decision made in the coming hours would shape the course of history.

CHAPTER 35

The atmosphere in the control room of the U-boat was tense, the crew working with a silent efficiency that spoke to their professionalism. Captain Bauer, stood at the periscope, scanning the dark waters for any sign of the enemy. He was deep in thought, contemplating their next move and their attack on America, when his Executive Officer, approached him with a serious expression.

"Captain Bauer, may I have a word with you in private?" the XO asked, his voice low and urgent.

Bauer glanced at him, noting the unusual gravity in his XO's demeanor. "Of course, Heinrich. Let's step into my quarters."

They made their way to the small, cramped captain's quarters, the door closing behind them with a soft click. Bauer gestured for Heinrich to sit, but the XO remained standing, his posture rigid with tension.

"What is it, Heinrich?" Bauer asked, his eyes narrowing.

"Sir, there are rumors circulating among the crew," Heinrich began, his voice barely above a whisper. "Rumors that Hitler is dead and that the war is lost. They say we're fighting for a lost cause."

Bauer's expression hardened, his jaw tightening. "And where did these rumors originate?"

"I'm not sure, Captain. But they're spreading fast. The men are growing anxious. Some are questioning our mission and what we're still doing out here."

Bauer was silent for a moment, his mind racing. He had suspected that morale was wavering, but this was more serious than he had anticipated. The crew's belief in their cause was essential to maintaining discipline and order on the boat. If these rumors continued to spread, it could undermine everything.

"Thank you for bringing this to my attention, Heinrich," Bauer said finally. "We cannot allow these rumors to fester. I will address the crew personally and put an end to this nonsense."

Heinrich nodded, relieved. "Yes, sir. I think that's the right course of action. The men trust you. They need to hear from you directly."

Bauer stood, his decision made. "Gather the men in the mess hall. I'll speak to them in ten minutes."

"Yes, Captain," Heinrich replied, snapping to attention before exiting the quarters to carry out the order.

Bauer took a deep breath, steeling himself for the task ahead. He knew that maintaining the crew's morale was crucial, especially now when their mission was more critical than ever. He would have to strike a delicate balance between quelling the rumors and keeping the men focused on their duty.

A few minutes later, Bauer entered the mess hall, where the crew had assembled, their faces a mix of curiosity and unease. He stepped up to the front, his presence commanding silence.

"Men," Bauer began, his voice strong and steady, "I have heard whispers among you. Whispers that our Führer is dead and that the war is lost. I am here to tell you that these are nothing but baseless rumors, designed to sow discord and weaken our resolve."

He paused, letting his words sink in. "Our mission remains unchanged. We are soldiers of the Reich, and we will continue to carry out our orders with the same dedication and professionalism that has always defined us. The fate of our Fatherland rests on our shoulders, and we will not falter."

The men listened intently, their expressions shifting from doubt to determination. Bauer could see the impact of his words, the resolve returning to their eyes.

"Trust in your training, trust in your comrades, and trust in our mission," Bauer continued. "We will see this through to the end, whatever it may bring. Dismissed."

As the crew dispersed, Bauer felt a sense of relief. He had managed to calm their fears for now. But he knew that the real test was yet to come. They were in uncharted waters, both literally and figuratively, and the challenges ahead would require all of his leadership and strength.

Returning to the control room, Bauer resumed his post, his mind already working on their next move. The war might be lost, but their fight was far from over. And as long as he was in command, he would ensure that his men remained focused and ready for whatever lay ahead.

Catching the XO's attention, Captain Bauer subtly motioned for him to step outside the control room, away from the crew's earshot. They moved to a secluded corner of the narrow passageway, where Bauer leaned in close, his voice low and icy.

"Heinrich, I know where these rumors are coming from," Bauer began, his eyes hardening with resolve. "They must be stopped. Quietly and without drawing attention, you need to eliminate Ingrid. We will dispose of her body when we surface to release our weapon on America."

The XO met Bauer's gaze and nodded grimly. "Understood, Captain," he replied. Without another word, he turned and made his way through the tight corridors of the U-boat, his mind focused on the task ahead.

Ingrid was being held in a small, locked room near the aft of the vessel, a makeshift cell hastily prepared when she was brought aboard. As Heinrich approached, he could hear the faint sounds of her pacing inside, the echo of her footsteps against the metal floor resonating in the confined space.

He paused for a moment outside the door, steeling himself. Ingrid had been a valuable informant, but her knowledge was now a threat to their mission. He knew what had to be done, even if it weighed heavily on his conscience.

He unlocked the door and stepped inside, closing it quietly behind him. Ingrid stopped pacing and turned to face him, her eyes filled with a mix of fear and defiance.

"I thought it was Hans with some food and water," she said, her voice trembling slightly. "What's going on? Why are you here?"

Heinrich took a deep breath, his expression neutral. "The rumors you've been spreading are jeopardizing our mission."

Ingrid's eyes widened in realization, and she took a step back. "Please, you don't have to do this. I can keep quiet, I promise."

But Heinrich shook his head, his resolve unwavering. "It's too late for that. You've already said too much. I have my orders."

Before she could react, Heinrich moved swiftly, his training and experience taking over. He grabbed her from behind, one arm around her neck, the other hand covering her mouth to stifle any cries for help.

Ingrid struggled desperately, her fingers clawing at his arm, but he held firm, his grip like iron.

The struggle was brief but intense. Within moments, Ingrid's movements slowed, then ceased altogether. He felt her body go limp in his arms, and he carefully lowered her to the floor, his heart pounding in his chest.

For a moment, he stood there in the silence, the reality of what he had done sinking in. He had followed orders, but it did not lessen the weight of his actions. He knew that in war, such decisions were necessary, but it did not make them any easier to bear.

He composed himself, ensuring no trace of the struggle remained. He would dispose of Ingrid's body as ordered when they surfaced, but for now, he had to return to his duties. With a final glance at Ingrid's lifeless form, he locked the room and walked back to the control room, his face a mask of stoic determination.

As he re-entered the control room, Captain Bauer glanced at him, a silent question in his eyes. Heinrich gave a slight nod, confirming the deed was done. Bauer nodded in return, turning his attention back to their mission. The U-boat continued its silent journey through the depths, the crew unaware of the grim task that had just been carried out to ensure their mission remained on course.

CHAPTER 36

The President sat in the Oval Office, the weight of the world pressing heavily on his shoulders. The devastation of London and Moscow hung over him like a dark cloud, and he knew the situation was growing increasingly dire. As he reviewed the latest intelligence reports, the door opened and his Chief of Staff, David, entered, his expression unusually tense.

"Mr. President," David said, his voice urgent. "There's someone from the Pentagon here to see you. He says he has a possible solution to the U-boat situation. He insists it's critical and must be discussed immediately."

The President nodded, setting the reports aside. "Send him in."

David stepped out briefly and returned with a middle-aged man in a crisp military uniform, his face lined with concern and determination. The man approached the President and saluted sharply.

"Mr. President, I'm Colonel John Reynolds assigned to the Pentagon," he began, his voice steady. "What I'm about to disclose may cost me my career, but I believe it is necessary to inform you of a top-secret device that could help us locate and neutralize the rogue U-boat."

The President gestured for him to continue, his curiosity piqued. "Go on, Colonel Reynolds."

Reynolds took a deep breath, his eyes locking onto the President's. "Sir, a year ago, we developed a top-secret device installed on one of our military satellites. This device was designed to detect and neutralize stealth technology. While it was never officially acknowledged, it has the capability to locate even the most advanced invisible submarines."

The President leaned forward, his interest intensifying. "Are you saying this device can find the U-boat and neutralize it?"

"Yes, Mr. President," Reynolds replied. "The device can pinpoint the exact location of the U-boat, despite its stealth capabilities. Moreover, it can emit a targeted EMP pulse that would disable the submarine's electrical systems, rendering it inoperable."

The room fell silent as the President processed the information. The stakes were incredibly high, and this revelation could be a turning point in the crisis.

"Why wasn't I informed about this earlier?" the President asked, his tone a mix of frustration and hope.

Reynolds hesitated, his gaze dropping briefly before he continued. "Sir, the device is part of a highly classified project, known only to a select few within the Pentagon. It's code name is '*Reveal*'. Its existence is a closely guarded secret due to the sensitive nature of its capabilities," he explained. "But given the current threat, I believe it's imperative that we use every available resource to prevent further attacks, and…"

He stopped, a look of unease crossing his face.

"And what? Please go on," the President said sternly, sensing there was more to be revealed.

Reynolds took another deep breath, his voice lowering. "Frankly, Mr. President, some members of the Pentagon still support the former president and will do anything they can to sabotage your administration. This device, and the knowledge of its capabilities, have been kept from you partly due to their influence."

The President's expression darkened, a mixture of anger and resolve forming in his eyes. "Are you telling me that internal politics have been jeopardizing national security?"

Reynolds nodded, his face etched with concern. "Yes, sir. That is exactly what I'm saying. And it's why I felt compelled to bring this information directly to you, despite the personal risk. Our country is facing an unprecedented threat, and we need to put aside any political differences to address it effectively."

The President stood, extending his hand to Reynolds. "Thank you, Colonel. Your courage and integrity are commendable. We need to act swiftly. I want you to coordinate with my National Security Advisor and get this device operational immediately. Until I get this rogue submarine neutralized, if you receive any type of blowback, you are to notify me immediately. I think it is time for a total cleaning of the house in the Pentagon."

Reynolds saluted again. "Yes, sir. I'll get on it right away."

As Reynolds left the room, the President turned to David. "Make sure our allies are informed and prepared. We may have a solution, but we need to be ready for any outcome."

David nodded, already moving to implement the President's directives. The President returned to his desk, a glimmer of hope piercing through the darkness. The next few hours would be critical, and he knew they had to act decisively to bring this crisis to an end.

**

"Captain, in nine hours we will be in range of the east coast of the United States," the helmsman shouted over the hum of the control room.

Captain Bauer glanced at his watch, calculating the time in his head. "Very well," he replied, his voice calm and measured. He turned to his Executive Officer, Lieutenant Heinrich Krüger. "I'm going to get some sleep. I will relieve you at 0200 hours."

"Understood, Captain," Krüger responded, nodding. Just as Bauer was about to leave the communications area, the sonar operator's voice cut through the tense atmosphere.

"Captain, sonar contact! Enemy submarine detected, bearing 345 degrees, moving southwest at 12 knots."

Bauer's eyes narrowed as he quickly assessed the situation. "Helmsman, take her down to 15 meters. Remain on course," he ordered, his tone firm and unyielding. He turned back to the XO. "They're still in the dark as to our exact location, but let's not take any chances."

"Helmsman, descending to 15 meters," the helmsman confirmed, deftly adjusting the controls. The submarine's descent was smooth, the only sound the creaking of the hull as it adjusted to the new depth.

"Leveling off at 15 meters, Captain," the helmsman reported moments later.

"Good," Bauer responded, his gaze fixed on the sonar display.

"Captain," the sonar operator's voice came again, "the enemy sub is passing over us. No change in her course or speed. The sound is drifting off. She is out of range."

A collective sigh of relief seemed to ripple through the control room, but Bauer remained stoic. "Maintain current depth and course. Keep monitoring their position," he instructed.

Krüger nodded, his expression serious. "We'll stay vigilant, Captain."

Bauer gave one last look at the sonar screen before turning to leave. "Remember, Heinrich, our mission is paramount. We can't afford any mistakes."

Krüger nodded again, his eyes reflecting the weight of their task. "Understood, Captain. We'll be ready."

As Bauer made his way to his quarters, the tension in the control room remained palpable. Every crew member was acutely aware of the stakes. They were on the brink of a critical moment, one that could determine the outcome of their mission and the fate of countless lives.

In his quarters, Bauer lays down, his mind racing despite his exhaustion. He looks at a picture of his family thinking of the good times in Germany before the war. He knew the coming hours would be some of the most crucial of his career. Closing his eyes, he forced himself to rest, knowing that he would need every ounce of his strength and focus for what lay ahead.

CHAPTER 37

The President's office, usually a symbol of calm and authority, was now a theater of tension. The President, a man known for his steely resolve, paced behind his desk, his face etched with frustration. The Joint Chiefs of Staff, the highest-ranking military officers in the country, stood in a line, their expressions a mix of guilt and apprehension.

"How the hell did you think you could hide something of this magnitude from me?" the President's voice was a low growl, his anger barely contained. "A secret satellite? 'Reveal'? And you kept it from your Commander-in-Chief? This action borders on treason."

General Harrison, the Chairman of the Joint Chiefs, stepped forward, attempting to explain. "Mr. President, we believed it was in the nation's best interest to maintain operational security—"

"Operational security?" the President interrupted, his voice rising. "This is not about some covert operation! This is about a rogue submarine which has launched two successful missile attacks into the heart of London and Moscow. And you thought it was wise to keep me in the dark?"

The room fell silent, the weight of the President's words hanging heavily in the air. The Joint Chiefs exchanged uneasy glances, knowing there was no justification that could appease their furious leader.

"General Harrison. You're dismissed," the President said coldly, his tone final. "And take your cronies with you. Consider your positions vacated immediately."

Stunned, the officers hesitated for a moment before saluting and filing out of the room. The door closed behind them with a soft thud, leaving the President alone with only a few officers who stood at attention, including Colonel John Reynolds, who the President focused on with a smile. He took a deep breath, trying to calm the storm of emotions swirling within him.

"Does anyone else want to hide things from the President?" No one answered. "Then let's proceed."

The National Security Advisor, Sarah Mitchell, entered the room, accompanied by Dr. Emily Harper, the chief scientist behind the 'Reveal' satellite. They approached the President's desk with a sense of urgency.

"Mr. President," Sarah began, "I know this has been a difficult day, but we need to move quickly. Dr. Harper is here to brief you on 'Reveal's' capabilities."

The President nodded, gesturing for everyone to sit. "Let's hear it."

Dr. Harper, a woman in her early forties with sharp intellect and a composed demeanor, opened a secure laptop on the President's desk. She brought up an image of the Earth, with a bright red dot pulsating in the middle of the Atlantic Ocean.

"Mr. President," she began, "the 'Reveal' satellite was designed for deep ocean surveillance. Its advanced sensors can detect and track underwater anomalies with unprecedented precision. This red dot represents U-boat 420."

The President leaned in, his interest piqued. "How accurate is this information?"

"Extremely accurate, sir," Harper replied. "We've been monitoring the submarine since it surfaced to launch the rocket at Moscow. We can track its movements in real-time and predict its potential courses."

Sarah Mitchell added, "We need to act swiftly. We have a narrow window to intercept the submarine before it reaches its next target."

The President's mind raced, weighing the options. The revelation of 'Reveal's' capabilities was a game-changer, but it also presented an opportunity to avert a catastrophic event. "What is the U-boat's present course?"

Dr. Harper hesitated before answering. "Mr. President, the U-boat is heading towards our east coast."

"Get me Admiral Collins," he ordered, referring to the head of the Navy. "We need to mobilize our fastest ships and submarines. And inform our NATO allies. This isn't just an American problem; it's a global threat. Get everyone we need in the war room ASAP.

As his team sprang into action, the President stood by the window, looking out at the White House lawn. The weight of the responsibility he bore felt heavier than ever. The next steps would be critical, not just for the safety of the nation, but for the future of global stability.

In that moment, the President knew that the fate of the world rested on their ability to outmaneuver a determined enemy lurking beneath the ocean's surface.

**

The dimly lit control room of U-boat 420 was filled with a tense anticipation. The hum of the engines and the soft beeping of the sonar were the only sounds, underscoring the gravity of their mission. Captain Bauer stood at the helm, his eyes fixed on the navigational charts, his mind calculating their approach.

"Captain, helm," the officer at the navigation console reported, breaking the silence. "We are one hour from our optimum range to launch."

Captain Bauer nodded, his expression steely and resolute. "Very well. Continue on our present course. When we are nearly at the outer marker of our launch zone, notify me so we can surface and prepare the rocket."

"Aye, aye, Captain," the helmsman responded with crisp efficiency, his hands steady on the controls.

Bauer turned to his XO, Lieutenant Commander Dietrich, who was monitoring the status of the torpedoes and the rocket. "Dietrich, ensure all systems are ready for launch. We cannot afford any mistakes."

Dietrich nodded, his face serious. "All systems are green, Captain. The rocket is primed and ready for deployment."

Captain Bauer allowed himself a brief moment to consider the enormity of their task. Their mission had already taken them across perilous waters, and now they were on the brink of executing an operation that could change the course of the war. Failure was not an option.

"Helm, maintain silent running. We don't want to alert any nearby patrols," Bauer ordered. "And prepare the crew for battle stations. We must be ready for any contingency."

The helmsman acknowledged the order, and a quiet buzz spread through the submarine as the crew prepared for the critical phase of their mission. The tension was palpable, but the men moved with the precision and discipline that had been drilled into them through countless hours of training and experience.

As the minutes ticked by, Bauer's thoughts returned to their objective. The rocket they carried and its success would hinge not only on their skill but also on a fair amount of luck. But Bauer had faith in his crew and their ability to see the mission through.

Finally, the helmsman spoke again, his voice steady. "Captain, we are approaching the outer marker of our launch zone."

Captain Bauer straightened, his eyes sharp. "Very well. Bring us to periscope depth and prepare to surface. XO, initiate the launch sequence for the rocket. Let's make history, gentlemen."

"Aye, aye, Captain," Dietrich replied, his hands moving swiftly over the controls.

The submarine began its slow ascent, the water pressure easing as they neared the surface. Bauer watched the depth gauge intently, every second feeling like an eternity.

"Surface the boat," he ordered, and the helmsman complied, bringing the U-boat up into the night air.

As the submarine broke the surface, the crew moved with practiced efficiency, opening the rocket housing and preparing the missile for launch. Bauer stepped onto the bridge, the cold wind biting at his face as he surveyed the dark ocean around them.

"XO, now is the time to get rid of our guest," the Captain ordered.

"Yes, Captain. I will get her body." Without fanfare, Ingrid's corpse was dropped over the side.

"Rocket is ready for launch, Captain," Dietrich reported from below.

Bauer took a deep breath, his gaze fixed on the horizon. "Launch the rocket."

The crew executed the command with precision, and moments later, the night sky was illuminated by the fiery trail of the rocket as it soared toward its target. The men watched in awe and trepidation, knowing that their actions could determine the fate of nations.

As the rocket disappeared from view, Bauer ordered the submarine to dive once more. "Take us back down. Set course for the United States. Our mission is far from over."

"Aye, aye, Captain," the helmsman responded, and the U-boat began its descent back into the depths, the crew ready for whatever lay ahead.

Captain Bauer stood resolute, his mind focused on the challenges to come. They had made their mark on history, but the war was not yet won. With steely determination, he prepared his crew for the next phase of their perilous journey.

CHAPTER 38

The war room in the White House was a hive of frenetic energy. The President stood at the center, surrounded by his top advisors, military officers, and the constant hum of communication devices. The large screen on the wall displayed a live feed from the 'Reveal' satellite, its data updating in real-time.

"Mr. President, the V-4 rocket has launched," an aide reported, his voice urgent.

The President's eyes narrowed as he watched the screen, the gravity of the situation settling heavily on his shoulders. "Get me Admiral Collins," he ordered, his voice firm.

A few moments later, Admiral Collins appeared on the main screen, the background of his naval command center bustling with activity. "Mr. President," he acknowledged with a salute.

"Admiral, the V-4 rocket has been launched," the President stated. "We need to shoot it down before it reaches its target. Use the 'Reveal' satellite."

"Understood, Mr. President," Collins responded. He turned to his team, issuing rapid commands. "Prepare to engage the 'Reveal' satellite. Target the V-4 rocket."

In the war room, the tension was palpable. The President's National Security Advisor, Sarah Mitchell, and Dr. Emily Harper, the chief scientist behind 'Reveal,' stood by the President's side, their faces set with determination.

Dr. Harper quickly connected her secure laptop to the main console, bringing up the control interface for the 'Reveal' satellite. "Mr. President, we have a lock on the rocket's trajectory," she announced.

"Shoot it down," the President commanded, his voice unwavering.

Harper's fingers flew over the keyboard, inputting the necessary commands. High above the Earth, the 'Reveal' satellite adjusted its position, its advanced sensors locking onto the rapidly ascending V-4 rocket. Within seconds, a powerful laser beam, invisible to the naked eye, fired from the satellite, piercing the atmosphere with pinpoint accuracy.

On the screen, the red dot representing the V-4 rocket flared brightly as the laser struck. The rocket detonated in a spectacular explosion, its fiery remains scattered across the sky. A collective sigh of relief echoed through the war room, but Thompson knew the situation was far from resolved.

"Good work, Dr. Harper," he said, his voice tempered with caution. "Admiral Collins, we need to now concentrate on the U-boat. What's the status of U-boat 420?"

**

Deep beneath the surface of the Atlantic, Captain Bauer and his crew felt the shockwave of the explosion ripple through the submarine. The lights flickered, and alarms blared as the U-boat rocked violently.

"Report!" Bauer demanded, his voice cutting through the chaos.

"Captain, we need to surface to assess the damage," Lieutenant Commander Dietrich responded, his face pale. "We've lost contact with the rocket."

Bauer clenched his jaw, understanding the implications. "Helm, bring us to periscope depth. We need to see what we're dealing with."

"Aye, aye, Captain," the helmsman replied, adjusting the controls.

The submarine began its slow ascent, the tension among the crew palpable. As they neared periscope depth, Bauer took his position at the periscope, raising it above the waterline. His heart sank as he saw the plume of smoke and debris marking the site of the explosion.

"Surface the boat," Bauer ordered, his voice heavy with frustration. "XO, prepare the damage assessment team. We need to know exactly what happened."

The U-boat broke the surface, and Bauer stepped onto the bridge, the cold wind biting at his face. He scanned the horizon, the reality of their situation sinking in. The rocket had failed to reach its target.

"Captain, we've detected residual energy signatures," Dietrich reported, joining him on the bridge. "It appears the rocket was intercepted and destroyed."

Bauer's mind raced. "How? The Allies must have some advanced technology to counter our attack. "This changes everything," he muttered, more to himself than anyone else. "We need to regroup and reassess our strategy."

"Captain, what are your orders?" Dietrich asked, his voice tinged with concern.

Bauer turned to face his crew, his determination unwavering. "We continue our mission. Set a new course for our secondary target, Washington D.C. We may have been thwarted once, but we will not be defeated. Prepare the crew for combat readiness. This war is far from over."

"Aye, aye, Captain," Dietrich and the crew responded in unison, their resolve matching their leader's.

As the U-boat descended once more into the depths, Bauer knew they were facing an uphill battle.

But he also knew that the true test of their strength was just beginning. They would adapt, overcome, and continue their fight, no matter the odds.

**

"Mr. President, the U-boat has set a new course. It is heading towards Washington, D.C.," Admiral Collins stated, his tone urgent and grave.

The President paused for a moment, deep in thought, before addressing the room. He turned to Dr. Lawrence, Dr. Souza, and Dr. Mueller. "You three were instrumental in locating the U-boat. Dr. Souza, Dr. Mueller, you are both highly regarded historians. We face a critical decision.

On one hand, I have the option to strike the submarine with an EMP blast, which would limit its capabilities to surfacing or diving. If we can establish communication with the U-boat commander, we might persuade him to surrender."

"On the other hand, every second we allow that lunatic to operate off our coast increases the risk of him launching another rocket or something even more destructive. I'm open to suggestions."

Dr. Souza stepped forward, his voice steady and persuasive. "Mr. President, Captain Bauer is a professional soldier. He might be open to reason, especially if he understands that the war he is fighting is over. If we appeal to his sense of duty and honor, we could prevent further conflict and bloodshed."

Dr. Mueller added, "Historically, many of these officers were not fanatics. They were following orders within the chain of command. If we offer them a way out that ensures their safety, they might see surrender as the best option."

The President nodded thoughtfully. "Admiral Collins, do we have the capability to monitor the U-boat and, if necessary, use 'Reveal' to neutralize it?"

"Yes, Mr. President," Collins replied. "We can maintain real-time surveillance and are ready to engage at your command."

"Alright," the President said decisively. "Let's attempt to make contact. Dr. Souza and Dr. Mueller, join me in addressing Captain Bauer."

A single-engine plane flew over the U-boat. Bauer, standing on the conning tower, watched as it dropped some type of float into the water before departing. He did not consider it a threat since it did not seem dangerous.

Soon a voice cracked on the speaker bobbing up and down in the sea.

"To U-boat 420. This is the President of the United States."

"Captain of U-boat 420. Please acknowledge," a voice crackled over the radio.

"This is Captain Bauer of U-boat 420. To whom am I speaking?"

"This is the President of the United States."

"Where is President Roosevelt? Is this an American trick?"

"Captain, I can assure you this is not a trick. The war you fought in is over. Germany has surrendered. Any further aggression will result in your immediate destruction. However, if you surrender, you and your crew will be treated humanely. I urge you to consider your position carefully."

"Again, where is President Roosevelt?" Bauer asked.

"President Roosevelt died on April 12, 1945. We are in the year 2024. Many decades have passed since Adolf Hitler was in power. The Germany you and your crew knew is in the past."

There was a long pause, filled with static and tension. Finally, Bauer responded, "Mr. President, I will discuss your offer with my crew."

CHAPTER 39

Bauer descended into the U-boat and gathered his senior officers and crew in the narrow confines of the control room. The weight of the moment was palpable, the air thick with tension and the unspoken fears of the men.

"Gentlemen," Bauer began, his voice steady but somber, "we have just received a communication from the President of the United States. He claims that the war is over, that Germany has surrendered. He offers us humane treatment if we surrender, but warns that any further aggression will lead to our destruction."

The men exchanged uneasy glances. Bauer continued, "I know this is difficult to believe. It feels like only yesterday that we were chosen by the Führer himself for this mission. We took a blood oath to our Fatherland, to fight and die for Germany."

The XO spoke up, his voice reflecting the inner conflict of many. "Captain, if what they say is true, then we are fighting a war that has already ended. But we have our orders, and our oath..."

Bauer nodded, understanding the turmoil in his crew. "I understand. But we must decide what is best for our country. We can choose to surrender and live, or we can continue our mission and possibly die. We have to make this decision together."

Silence fell over the control room as each man grappled with the gravity of their situation. Finally, the XO broke the silence. "Captain, we took an oath. We were chosen for this mission because we are the best. Our duty is clear."

One by one, the officers voiced their agreement. Their loyalty to their Fuhrer, mission and their country was unwavering. "We cannot surrender," said Lieutenant Meyer, his voice resolute. "We owe it to our comrades, to our families, and to the Fatherland to complete our mission. Sieg Hiel!"

Bauer looked at his men, pride swelling in his chest. "Very well. We stand united. We will not surrender. We will complete our mission or die trying."

A sense of resolve filled the cramped space of the U-boat as the men returned to their stations, ready to face whatever came next. Bauer took a deep breath, knowing the path they had chosen was fraught with danger.

"While I continue my conversation with the American president, quickly prepare the rocket for launch."

He returned to shout at the bobbing speaker, his voice steady. "Mr. President, we have considered your offer, but our mission is not complete. We cannot surrender. We took a blood oath to our Führer to die for our Fatherland. He personally selected us for this mission."

The war room watched in tense silence as the U-boat crew quickly moved to ready another V-4 rocket for launch. President Trump's face hardened with resolve.

"Captain, many presidents have come and gone since the end of World War II. If you and your crew had family members, they too, might have passed on. But many people, including your friends and relatives, are most likely still alive, hoping to learn of your fate."

Bauer's determination only seemed to deepen. "I appreciate your words, Mr. President, but our duty is clear."

The President talks to Admiral Collins, his voice firm and unwavering. "Admiral Collins, we cannot allow this threat to continue. Destroy the U-boat."

"Understood, Mr. President," Collins replied. He turned to his team, issuing the final command. "Engage 'Reveal' and target U-boat 420. Prepare for immediate strike."

High above, the 'Reveal' satellite adjusted its position, its sensors locking onto the submarine. A powerful laser beam fired, piercing the atmosphere with deadly precision. On the screen, the war room watched as U-boat 420 was hit, the explosion tearing through the hull and sending it to the ocean floor.

A heavy silence filled the room as the enormity of their actions sank in. President Trump looked at his advisors and military officers, a somber expression on his face. "We did what we had to do to protect our nation. Now, let's ensure we're prepared for any further threats."

As the team sprang into action to secure the area and assess any further risks, the President stood by the window, looking out at the White House lawn. The weight of his decisions bore heavily on him, but he knew they had averted a catastrophe and safeguarded the future.

In that moment, the President realized the true cost of leadership in times of unprecedented danger and the profound responsibility of safeguarding peace in a volatile world.

**

Lena and Alex opted for room service in their hotel room. They would fly back to Bergen in the morning, but both realized that it would be anti-climatic given everything that had occurred.

"What do you think happened to Ingrid?" Lena asked, looking at the hotel room service menu.

"My gut tells me that the Nazis eliminated her way before the U-boat was destroyed. I bet the *Norwegian* government will just sweep her possible Russian agent accusations under the rug."

"I can't help wondering if there are other weapons concealed on orders of Hitler, just waiting to be put in motion," Lena said.

"If there are, I sure hope we don't discover them," Alex said.

OTHER BOOKS BY THE AUTHOR:

JEANNIE LOOMIS THRILLER NOVELS:

Ark of the Covenant – Raid on the Church of Our Lady Mary of Axion

Star Chamber

Forgotten Plans

House of Special Purpose

Time Game

Thin Blue Line

The Fourth Reich

Black Heart/Black Cell

The Phantom Train

Rollercoaster

Snow Angel

Relics of Redemption

HORROR NOVELS:

House on Haunted Hill Resurrection

The Tingler

13 Ghosts Awakened

Beneath the Earth

Carnival of Lost Souls

The Birds Return

Ice Creature

NOVELLA

The Hidden Workshop

COMING SOON:

The Gold Enigma – 15th Loomis novel

Back to the Black Lagoon – horror

www.ingramcontent.com/pod-product-compliance
Lightning Source LLC
Chambersburg PA
CBHW020559310726
48979CB00008B/1276/J

* 9 7 9 8 9 9 0 7 2 5 4 4 7 *